"Do . . . quavering. She hadn't anticipated things getting this heavy this fast. She felt ill prepared to deal with it.

He shrugged helplessly. "I'm still getting acquainted with the woman you've become, Callie. But I'm pretty sure that if I were given half a chance, I'd fall in love with you all over again, even if it wasn't the smartest thing to do."

"Oh, Sam, I . . ." Words simply failed her. Her throat tightened, and tears of some very strong emotion threatened to spill from her eyes.

Sam went to her then and put his arms around her. "Don't cry, darlin'," he said, rubbing her back.

She settled against him, listening to the soothing, steady beat of his heart. The familiarity of his embrace was like a balm to her soul. It was almost like they'd never been apart.

"Mmm."

"Unless you stop me, I'm going to pick you up and carry you into the bedroom and have my way with you."

"I won't stop you," she said, her words muffled against his chest. "Let's finish what we started all those years ago."

WHAT ARE *LOVESWEPT* ROMANCES?

They are stories of true romance and touching emotion. We believe those two very important ingredients are constants in our highly sensual and very believable stories in the LOVE-SWEPT line. Our goal is to give you, the reader, stories of consistently high quality that may sometimes make you laugh, sometimes make you cry, but are always fresh and creative and contain many delightful surprises within their pages.

Most romance fans read an enormous number of books. Those they truly love, they keep. Others may be traded with friends and soon forgotten. We hope that each LOVESWEPT romance will be a treasure—a "keeper." We will always try to publish

LOVE STORIES YOU'LL NEVER FORGET
BY AUTHORS YOU'LL ALWAYS REMEMBER

The Editors

BRIDES OF DESTINY: CALLIE'S COWBOY

KAREN LEABO

BANTAM BOOKS

NEW YORK · TORONTO · LONDON · SYDNEY · AUCKLAND

BRIDE OF DESTINY: CALLIE'S COWBOY

A Bantam Book / October 1996

ISBN 0-553-44540-5

Published simultaneously in the United States and Canada

PROLOGUE

On a warm April day in Destiny, Texas, the high-school spring carnival was in full swing. The scent of popcorn mingled with that of cotton candy, and the gymnasium echoed with whoops of conquest from the many games and the excited laughter of children.

Seventeen-year-old Callie Calloway couldn't enjoy any of it. Her heart was breaking into pieces.

"I'm sorry that's the way you feel, Callie," Sam said, his usual sunny smile absent. "But Uncle Ned needs me. He's in bad health, the spring calving hasn't gone well, and . . . we're talking about my whole future here. You understand that, don't you?"

Callie nodded, swallowing back the tears. For as long as she'd known Sam Sanger, he'd taken care of his family. He'd helped his great-uncle on a ranch in Nevada every summer and had given most of his salary to his parents to add to the meager income they earned from their own struggling farm. It had all seemed so noble to Callie, and that's one of the reasons she'd fallen in love with him.

He loved her, too, she knew. But just once, she wanted to come first. Was that too much to ask?

Apparently it was. Sam had moved heaven and earth to finish his high-school credits a month early so he'd be free to leave for Nevada for the summer. And now he'd just informed her that he was leaving before the senior prom.

"I'll understand if you want to go with another guy to the prom," he said. "But do we have to break up? I mean, aren't you overreacting?"

Callie shook her head. "I know you. You're going to stay up in Nevada for good this time. We might as well face that fact and go on."

"I'll be back," he said. "I'm learning all about ranching, and I'll come back and build up Mama and Daddy's farm, just like I always said I would. You wait, it'll be the prettiest—"

Callie covered her ears. "Please. Just go, Sam. I don't want to hear it anymore."

Sam shoved his thumbs into his jeans pockets. "Okay, Callie," he said, a little defiantly. "I'll go. But we're not through. Far from it."

He swaggered away, and Callie sniffed back her tears. She'd played her trump card, and it hadn't been enough. At least she knew where she fell on Sam's list of priorities.

She needed a distraction, something to do that would make her forget all about Sam. Her tear-blurry vision settled on a booth in the corner swathed in glittery red silk. Where had that come from?

The small booth featured a gold-lettered sign that read THEODORA, FORTUNE-TELLER.

Callie frowned and consulted her clipboard. There was no fortune-teller, Theodora or otherwise, on her list of attractions sanctioned by the carnival committee, and no one had told her about any last-minute additions.

"I'll get to the bottom of this," Callie murmured. A problem to solve would take her mind off Sam's desertion. She shoved a strand of her long dark hair behind her ear and pushed her glasses higher up on the bridge of her nose, ready for battle.

Still, even wearing her official-looking Carnival Committee/Student Division ID badge, she didn't want to confront Theodora alone. She needed reinforcements. She scanned the crowd, searching for her two fellow committee members.

Lana wasn't hard to find. All Callie had to do was look for the biggest crowd of boys, and Lana Walsh would be in the center. It would have been easy to feel jealous of the pretty blonde, except that her charm wasn't forced or calculated; it came naturally. She was a hard worker, too, when properly motivated.

Callie elbowed her way through the appreciative, hormone-driven males who were crowding around the table where Lana was selling tickets.

Lana looked up and smiled. "Oh, hi, Callie. Ticket sales are booming."

Exactly why Callie had put Lana in charge of tickets. She'd known that all the boys, at least, would buy handfuls from her.

"Mrs. Dingmeir can handle sales for a while," Callie said. "We have some official business to take care of."

One of the boys watching the exchange, a big, strapping football player named Bart Gaston, put his hand on top of Callie's head and exerted just enough backward pressure that she was forced to look up at him. "What kind of official business?"

Supremely annoyed, she ducked out of his grasp. "Nothing that concerns you, lunkhead." She turned her attention back to Lana. "Coming?"

"Sure." Lana smiled apologetically, then deftly maneuvered the crowd of boys to Mrs. Dingmeir's table.

"You shouldn't be so rude to Bart," Lana whispered as she and Callie left the group. "I think he's going to ask me to the prom. Has Sam asked you yet?"

The question made Callie's heart clench painfully. "Sam and I won't be going to the prom." Before Lana could interrogate her, she changed the subject. "Where's Millicent?" Millicent Whitney was the third on their student carnival committee.

"She's helping out with the face painting, remember? Honestly, speaking of not having a date for the prom . . . I mean, Millicent's not as plain as she thinks she is. If she would only try to meet some boys . . ."

"I know. But she's so darn shy."

"She's going to end up alone and lonely," Lana said sadly. "And that's really a shame. She's smart and nice, and she loves kids."

That much was evident. As the two girls approached the face-painting booth they found Millicent busily painting a unicorn onto a little girl's cheek. The child, about four, sat still as a stone, enthralled by the artist's soft voice as Millicent told her a story. She finished up just as she saw Callie and Lana approaching.

"Hi, how's it going?" Millicent lifted the child off the table where she'd been sitting and put her on the ground, sending her off to her father with a pat on the head.

"Fine with me," Lana said, "but Callie says we have official business to take care of."

Millicent looked to Callie for more of an explanation.

Callie turned and pointed to the silk-swathed booth. "Did y'all notice that?"

"The fortune-teller?" Millicent said. "What about her?"

"She's not on the list. Where'd she come from?"

The two other girls shrugged. "Does it matter?" Millicent asked.

"Of course it matters. She might have sneaked in here under false pretenses. She might be taking cash under the table."

"Callie, you're so suspicious," Lana admonished gently. "Probably Mr. Stipley simply forgot to tell us about her." Mr. Stipley was the principal of Destiny High School, and the carnival was his baby.

"I want to find out for sure," Callie said. "And I want you both to come with me."

Lana laughed. "All right. But if we find out she's legit, we all have to have our fortunes told. Agreed?"

The other two girls nodded reluctantly.

As they approached Theodora's booth Callie thought it odd that the fortune-teller had no takers. The carnival was crowded, and almost every attraction had a line in front of it. But Theodora, a darkly exotic woman dressed in a gypsy costume, sat behind a silk-draped table with a crystal ball in front of her, as if she'd been waiting just for these three customers.

Her wide, red-painted mouth spread into a smile. "Well, now, what do we have here? Did you come to find out which boy will ask you to the prom?"

Callie got a wiggly sensation down her spine. How odd that she and Lana had recently been discussing that very thing. "Actually, Miss, uh, Ms. Theodora, this is an official visit. I'm head of the Carnival Committee/Student Division, and these are my committee members." She consulted her clipboard, trying to look serious and severe. "You aren't on my list."

"My, aren't you the official one," Theodora said, still smiling. In an aside to the other two girls, she added, "I'll bet nothing gets by her, eh? She probably dots all her *i*'s and crosses the *t*'s."

Millicent covered her mouth to disguise her smile, and Lana laughed out loud, earning a scowl from Callie.

"You're the skeptical type," Theodora continued, looking at Callie. "You love to ask questions and you can't stand an unsolved mystery. You would make a very good newspaper reporter."

"H-how did you know that?" Callie asked. She'd already been accepted into the journalism program at Stockton University, the college around which the town of Destiny, Texas, had grown.

"I know all kinds of things," Theodora said mysteriously. "Would you like to hear more?"

"I'd like to hear who gave you permission to set up here," Callie persisted. "You're not on my—"

"Chill out, Callie," Lana said. "I'd like to hear more. Can you tell me who I'll go to the prom with?"

Theodora consulted her crystal ball, and Callie observed, fascinated despite herself. Out of habit, she pulled a small pad and pen from the back pocket of her jeans and began taking notes. She was always on the lookout for a good story for the school paper.

"I see you going to the prom with a football player," Theodora said.

Big stretch, Callie thought uncharitably. Someone with Lana's looks would naturally snag a football player.

Theodora looked up. "You have many talents, you know," she said. "I see you surrounded by flowers."

Lana giggled. "I hope that means Bart will bring me a big ol' corsage for the dance. Now, what about Millicent?" She dragged her friend forward. "Who's she gonna go with?"

Millicent sighed. "I don't need a fortune-teller to give me that answer. I won't be going."

Theodora peered into the ball. "I see you painting. You have such talent!"

Another big stretch, Callie thought. Millicent had paint smears all over her hands.

"I'll probably be painting the prom decorations," Millicent said glumly.

"Oh, who cares about this silly prom business," Lana interrupted. "We want to know who we're going to marry. Right?" She looked to the other two girls for confirmation.

"Gee, I'm not sure I want to know. . . ." Millicent said, but Theodora was already staring into her crystal ball.

The gypsy was silent a long time while the girls collectively held their breath. Then, unexpectedly, she looked up and began to recite a poem:

One will tarry, losing her chance at love;
The next will marry, but her spouse will rove;
A third will bury her man in a hickory grove;
But all will find marriage a treasure trove,
With a little help from above

Callie shivered, even though she knew this was all a bunch of silliness. She'd always harbored a secret worry that she and Sam would marry and that he would die, leaving her a widow. If the brutal ranch work didn't kill him, his rodeo bull riding would.

"The poem's nice, but it's not very helpful," Lana pointed out. "I want a name. How will I know my future husband when I meet him?"

Theodora smiled indulgently. "Everyone who has her fortune told by Theodora gets a souvenir. These mementos will help you recognize the man who will make you happy." She reached under the table and pulled out a cardboard box that appeared to be filled with gum-machine toys and other worthless stuff. She rummaged around in it for a moment, then held out her hand toward Callie.

Callie couldn't contain her curiosity. She accepted Theodora's gift. It was a plastic key chain in the shape of a cowboy boot.

Her skin broke out in goose bumps. How could the fortune-teller know about Sam? "I'm not marrying anyone who wears cowboy boots," she said firmly. Theodora merely gave her a knowing smile.

Lana frowned, obviously puzzled, at her gift from Theodora. It was a toy policeman's badge made of tin.

Theodora had to search a bit longer for something to give Millicent. She finally came up with a tiny brown glass bottle, the kind used for medicine a hundred years ago.

As the three girls stood contemplating their gifts Theodora quietly stood and walked to the back of her booth. Callie was the first to notice that she was gone. "Hey, where'd she go?"

Lana pointed to the wavering curtain in the rear of the booth. "Back there."

Callie barged forward, her skepticism returning with full force. If this pseudo-gypsy thought she was going to distract her with her mumbo jumbo and a worthless trinket . . .

She pulled back the curtain. No one was there. The girls stepped outside the booth, looked around corners, under tables. There was no sign of Theodora. Then Callie saw a flash of brightly colored silk vanishing through the back door of the gym. "This way!" she said to her friends, and they all three ran off in hot pursuit of the fortune-teller. But when they got outside, they couldn't find her.

"I knew it." Callie tried to catch her breath. "I knew she was some kind of charlatan."

"I didn't think she was so bad," Lana said. "She told our fortunes for free."

"We'll have to go to Mr. Stipley," Callie said. "Something's definitely fishy."

They went back into the gymnasium, but almost before the door slammed behind them, Callie came to a screeching halt and the other two girls ran into her. "Look." She pointed toward Theodora's booth—or rather, the place where Theodora's booth had stood a minute or two earlier. There was no sign of red silk or glitter. A dart game occupied the space.

The three girls looked at each other, their eyes wide with apprehension. Callie knew her friends were thinking what she was thinking—there was no way anyone could have moved Theodora's booth that quickly.

"D-did we just have a group hallucination?" Millicent asked, her voice a timid squeak.

Callie opened the hand in which she'd been clutching the key chain. It was still there. She could see that the other girls still held their souvenirs from their visit with Theodora. "I'm not sure what it was," Callie said. "But I don't think we should tell anyone about it."

"Agreed," the other two girls responded together. They all clasped hands, knowing that the secret they must keep would bind them to each other forever.

ONE

Callie hated covering funerals, but she hadn't trusted anyone on her staff to handle Johnny Sanger's send-off. She'd felt compelled to be there herself. Johnny's sensational death was the type of event that naturally led to gossip and speculation, but Callie had forbidden her reporters from pursuing the story. If anything beyond an objective accounting of the facts was to be written about the Sangers, she would be the one to do it.

Callie's chest tightened as her gaze focused on Sam, who sat with his family in a special section reserved for them on the opposite side of the closed casket. She couldn't see his face. He'd kept his head bowed during most of Reverend Snyder's endless eulogy, the oblique autumn sun glinting off his sun-bleached hair. She wondered if he'd seen her, and if he had, what he would think.

Then she had to laugh at herself. He had more important things on his mind than an ex-girlfriend. His father had just died, violently and unexpectedly, and he must be devastated. Though he lived far away, he was devoted to his parents. Callie suspected that the only reason the Sangers had held on to their farm was because Sam helped them out financially.

Her physical reaction to him was undeniable, even after all this time. Much to her chagrin, her breasts tingled, and she couldn't seem to get comfortable in her chair. True, they'd hardly spoken in years, but they'd once been involved in a rip-roaring, explosive relationship, complete with all the passionate declarations, tearful arguments, and lonely, anguished nights that often come with the territory of first love.

Callie tried to push those old memories aside. Whatever the ups and downs of their past, the Sanger family would always be special to her, and she wished there was some way she could lend her support. Just because she'd turned down Sam's marriage proposal didn't mean she'd stopped caring about him. They had always been there for each other in times of trouble.

The last eight years had been good to Sam. His body looked tough and solid beneath his dark blue suit, while his tanned skin contrasted with the crisp white shirt he wore.

His nervous hands fiddled with the bow at the back of his two-year-old daughter's dress. Callie wondered where Debra, Sam's wife, was.

Little Deana Sanger wiggled down from Sam's lap to play at his feet with a pink stuffed animal, oblivious to the fact that she was witnessing her grandfather's burial. A lump formed in Callie's throat, and she determinedly swallowed it back. That poor child would have to live the rest of her life with the knowledge that her grandfather had shot himself.

The police had ruled it suicide, anyway, and Callie had dutifully reported it as such. But something hadn't felt right about the story from the moment she'd first gotten the news of an accident at the Sanger farm.

She focused her attention on the rest of the family. Beverly, Sam's mother, looked grim and determined, as if all she wanted was to get through this tedious ceremony so she could go home and fall apart. Callie wondered how in the world she would get along without Johnny.

Beverly's older son, Will, sat next to her holding her hand. Callie didn't know Will very well, but from what Sam had told her over the years about his half brother, that was for the best. Will had been responsible for a fatal drunk-driving accident when he was in high school and had been in and out of jail ever since. The girl who'd died in the crash was the daughter of a prominent Destiny businessman, and the Sangers had never quite gotten over the scandal.

Will looked sober and respectable now, Callie thought, surreptitiously making a few notes in her notebook. His face was a mask of grief, his suit was properly somber, and his dark hair was cropped short and neatly combed. A slight woman with light brown hair in limp curls sat next to him, clinging to his arm. Callie assumed the woman was Will's wife, Tamra. Callie had never met her, but she'd read her name in the police report on Johnny's death. She was pretty in an ethereal way, but she looked wiped out.

No wonder, poor girl. She and Beverly had discovered the body.

The ceremony concluded, the coffin was lowered into the ground, and family members each tossed a bit of dirt onto the casket. Out of sheer habit, Callie leaned into the aisle, raised her camera, and caught a poignant image of little Deana solemnly letting a handful of dirt sift through her fingers into the yawning grave.

Still, hearing the click of the shutter, Sam looked up and scowled at Callie. She bit her lip and immediately put the camera away. Eight years ago, when she was in college, Sam had been hurt and angry at her decision not to marry him and move to Nevada. The few times she'd seen him since then had been uncomfortable, but she didn't want to believe that he truly disliked her.

Callie felt a hand on her shoulder. She turned and was surprised to see that her friend Millicent Jones had claimed the chair next to her.

"I had a feeling I might find you here," Millicent whispered. "I'm glad you're personally covering the funeral. I know you'll handle it with dignity. You did such a nice job with Ronnie's."

"Thanks," Callie mumbled. She was already on the verge of tears. She didn't need to think about Millicent's husband, Ronnie, who was buried not a hundred feet away in a shady spot between two hickory trees. She looked down at her feet, up at the puffy white clouds overhead—everywhere but at Millicent's pregnant stomach. At four months, she was starting to show.

The service ended. Callie and Millicent stood up along with everyone else as the attendees began to mill around and wander away. "Did you know Johnny Sanger?" Callie asked.

"Not well, but I know Beverly. I've bought eggs from their farm for ages. And of course I know Sam from when you two . . ."

Callie nodded.

"The crowd's thinning out," Millicent said. "Are you going to pay your respects to the family?"

Callie hesitated. She and Beverly Sanger had always gotten along well, even after Callie and Sam had broken up for the last time. But she didn't want to cause Sam any extra stress.

"Come on," Millicent urged. "I'll go with you. I was thinking of volunteering to baby-sit Sam's little girl, anyway, so while he's in town he can be free to help his mother."

Typical Millicent, Callie thought. Her own life was a tragedy in progress, yet she was always thinking about ways to ease someone else's burden. "I wonder where Sam's wife is," Callie asked, thinking aloud.

Millicent stopped. "Lord, Callie, you mean you don't know?"

"Know what?"

"They divorced more than a year ago. Debra left him and their baby."

"No way," Callie said flatly. "I'm the newspaper editor. I know everything."

"Apparently not everything. Beverly Sanger herself told me a few weeks ago." When Callie continued to stare, her mouth hanging open, Millicent added, "I just assumed you knew, and I didn't think it polite to bring it up."

Callie was floored. A small corner of her heart fluttered at the realization that Sam was free.

From the calculating look on Millicent's face, her thoughts were running along the same lines.

"Oh, no," Callie said.

"Now, what would it hurt for you to spend some time with him while he's in town, maybe get to know his daughter—"

"I'm not good with children," Callie interrupted. "Besides, it would hurt. Nothing has changed since we broke up."

"A lot's changed," Millicent argued. "And there's Theodora's predictions to think about."

"Don't start with that hocus-pocus stuff again—"

"You have to admit, the poem came true. Lana's husband 'roved,' I buried mine—"

"I know, I know, in a hickory grove, if two trees can count as a grove."

"And you tarried here in Destiny instead of moving to Nevada, missing your chance to marry Sam. But maybe it's not too late."

As they'd talked they'd gradually worked their way toward the Sanger family. Callie realized she wanted to pay her respects, regardless of her feelings for Sam or his for her. She owed it to Beverly.

As the two younger women approached, Beverly Sanger greeted them gracefully, accepting hugs from them both. She introduced them to Will and Tamra, who both politely shook their hands and thanked them for coming.

"Hey, I remember you," Will said to Callie. "Didn't you used to—"

Tamra loudly cleared her throat. "Not now, Will," she said, looking acutely embarrassed.

Beverly quickly jumped in. "And of course you both know Sam." She looked anxiously at her younger son, who was kneeling in front of the chair where Deana sat, helping her button her sweater.

"I'm so sorry—" Callie began as soon as he turned to look at her, but Sam cut her off.

"Are you going to run the picture of my little girl in the paper?" he asked, straightening to face her. His expression was hard and not the least bit welcoming.

"Sam!" Beverly scolded.

"I won't know which photo to run until I develop the film," Callie answered diplomatically. "Would it bother you?"

"I'm not especially comfortable with the publicity for Deana, that's all." His deep blue gaze focused totally on Callie. "Hasn't the town had enough to chew on with the way Dad died?"

Millicent stepped forward, rushing to take her friend's side. "Whatever Callie prints, she'll do it with taste. You really don't have to worry about that."

Some of the tension drained out of Sam as he looked curiously at Callie's defender. "Millicent, isn't it? From high school?"

"Yes."

"The fireman who died—he was your husband."

"Yes." Millicent's voice was barely a whisper. She shrank back.

Callie wished the ground could swallow them all up right about now. How could Sam be so insensitive?

"Look," she said, taking Millicent's arm, "this was a bad idea. We'll leave you all alone now."

"It wasn't a bad idea," Beverly objected. "Thank you both for coming. It means a lot. Some of us are running a bit low on manners at this point, that's all."

Callie gave Sam's mother a parting smile of gratitude before she and Millicent turned to make their escape. But as she started to step away, her slick-soled pumps skidded on the wet grass and her feet flew out from under her. She would have landed flat on her fanny if Sam hadn't reached out and caught her under the arms.

He didn't say a word, just helped her get steady on her feet. But he didn't have to speak. The physical contact between them sent sparks shooting all the way to Callie's toes. She felt her face flushing from more than embarrassment. She realized they hadn't touched, hadn't so much as shaken hands, in eight years—and she'd missed the feel of his touch. He'd once known how to send her straight to heaven with his caresses. The memories, so sudden and so acute, made her tremble inside.

"Thank you," she said politely as he released her. This time when she walked away, she looked down at her still-wobbly feet to make sure she didn't misstep.

Sam watched Callie walk away, momentarily hypnotized by the gentle sway of her hips beneath the somber business suit she wore. Her thick brown hair still hung past her shoulders, but today she'd tamed it back with a black bow. And she still wore glasses. He wondered how many people knew she didn't need them.

"Sam Sanger, I thought I raised you better than that," Beverly said. "Callie Calloway has been a friend of our family for years. You had no call to—"

"She came to the funeral as a reporter, not a friend." Sam picked up his sleepy-eyed daughter and propped her on his hip. "Don't tell me you've forgotten the mess that newspaper once made of our lives." His gaze slid over to Will and back. "And I don't like the idea of her taking pictures of Deana."

"She has a job to do, just like everyone else," Beverly said. "Besides, I for one wouldn't mind seeing a picture of a sweet little girl saying good-bye to her grandfather. I'd much prefer that to a picture of the pitiful widow with a handkerchief to her face."

"You're not a pitiful widow." Will slipped an arm around his mother's shoulders. "We'll get through this, Mother. It'll be okay. I'm here to help you."

Sam cast a jaundiced eye at his half brother. Will had never in his life helped anyone but himself. Still, Sam had to admit that he had been very supportive during the ordeal of the past few days, and even before Johnny's accident he'd shown signs of wanting to heal the family rift. He'd been out of prison for almost four months, paroled for good behavior, and claimed he was straightening out his life. He'd married a girl he'd been corresponding with in prison, and he even had a job he seemed to like at a paper recycling plant.

Maybe Will had changed, Sam thought, and it was his own cynical outlook that cast everyone in a bad light.

"The limo driver's waiting," Will said.

Sam realized that everyone else had left, even Reverend Snyder. One last limo ride to the farm, and the funeral would be over. Then Sam could concentrate on getting his mother's affairs in order. He intended to try to talk her into coming back to Nevada with him, at least for a visit.

"You should call poor Callie and tell her you don't really mind about the picture," Beverly said as she picked her way cautiously over the uneven grass in her high heels. "She would never take advantage of any situation to sell newspapers. She's not like that."

Sam snorted in disbelief. "Callie Calloway? The girl who once dressed up as a football player so she could get inside the boys' locker room and find out if we really had centerfold girls pinned up on the walls?"

"Oh, Sam, for heaven's sake, that was when she was in high school. She's matured a lot since then. You haven't lived here day in and day out, reading the paper. She's done a very responsible job since she took over as editor last year—the youngest editor the *Record*'s ever had, mind you. She covers every issue fairly, from both sides, and she's never too sensational."

"That remains to be seen. I think we all need to be cautious."

Sam had already read the accounts Callie had written of his father's death. So far the stories had been low-key, bare facts only. But Sam wasn't naive enough to think that would be the end of it. The people of Destiny were hungry for more information about Johnny Sanger. And Callie was the type to answer demands, fill needs, fill vacuums. She wouldn't let a past connection with the victim's son stand in the way of her career.

Callie yawned expansively as she waited for Millicent and Lana in a back booth at the Pie Pantry tearoom. The three women met for lunch every month, a tradition they'd started in high school. In the beginning they'd met to discuss their strange encounter with the mysterious fortune-teller Theodora, analyzing the incident endlessly, trying to extract some meaning from it. But eventually, as Theodora's predictions faded into a distant memory, the monthly lunches had become strictly social events.

Lana, who worked at the florist's shop next door, arrived first, but Millicent was right behind. They all placed their usual orders with the waitress, who knew them by name and always held the back booth open for their monthly meetings.

"You look tired," Millicent said to Callie when the waitress had gone.

"I was late at the paper last night," Callie explained, stifling another yawn. In truth, she'd been writing and rewriting the account of Johnny Sanger's funeral until her production manager had forced her to send the story to typesetting. She still wasn't happy with it.

"The story on the funeral was very nice," Millicent said, as if she'd just read Callie's mind. "I'm sure Sam will be pleased."

"Sam?" Lana's interest perked up as she buttered a roll.

"I'm not sure he'd be pleased with anything I did,"

Callie said dismissively. She turned to Lana. "How's Rob? Did he win his football game Friday night?" Rob was Lana's eight-year-old son.

"He fumbled twice."

"Callie, why won't you talk about Sam?" Millicent persisted. "I know you still have feelings for him. You're both free. Are you sure you don't want to get reacquainted?"

Callie shook her head. She knew Millicent was only speaking out of concern, but thoughts of Sam brought back too many painful memories.

Millicent sighed. "How is Theodora's prediction ever going to come true if you won't get within a hundred feet of a cowboy?"

"Theodora?" Lana looked quizzically at Millicent. "We haven't talked about her in years. I thought we all agreed to forget about her."

"That was before her predictions started coming true," Millicent said. "Callie became a newspaper reporter, just like Theodora said, and I became an artist. Now Lana is surrounding herself with flowers."

"Hey, that's right!" Lana said. "Theodora did say she saw me surrounded by flowers. I'd forgotten about that."

"Then there's the poem," Millicent continued. "She had us pegged there, agreed?"

"She made vague predictions," Callie argued.

"How'd she know about the hickory trees?" Millicent persisted. "That burial plot's been in Ronnie's family for fifty years."

Callie shrugged. She'd thought that Millicent had deliberately picked a plot with hickory trees, a self-fulfilling prophecy. "I'll agree she's made a few lucky guesses. But none of us have married the men she predicted for us."

"Ronnie was a paramedic," Millicent said. "That's close enough to the doctor she chose for me." She smiled mischievously at Callie. "And Theodora must have had Sam in mind for you. It's not too late."

"Oh, please. Like he wants anything to do with me. And I'm not moving to Nevada, anyway. Besides, I'd have to deal with Deana, and I'm not the stepmother type."

Lana laughed in between bites of her roll. "We hear you, Callie. How many more excuses can you come up with? But I never have understood what you have against Nevada. I wouldn't mind going to live on a big ol' ranch."

"Then you marry Sam," Callie teased.

"Oh, no, I couldn't do that. I'm waiting for my policeman."

Millicent frowned disapprovingly at her friends' ridicule of a subject she took quite seriously.

Their food arrived, and the conversation turned to more mundane matters. But Millicent didn't want to let the matter of Theodora's predictions drop. "Callie, won't you at least consider spending some time with Sam while he's in town? Y'all have both grown up a lot. Things might be different."

Callie pushed aside her half-eaten turkey sandwich. "Millicent, I know you want everyone to be happy, but I'm not interested in Sam anymore." Never mind that not an hour had gone by in the last twenty-four that she hadn't thought about how his hands had felt on her. "He means nothing to me."

"Well, in that case, here comes nothing," Lana said in a wary voice.

Callie followed her friend's gaze. Sure enough, there was Sam Sanger walking through the restaurant, bearing down on their table. His work jeans and battered boots looked out of place in the frilly, feminine tearoom.

"Oh, no," she murmured, bowing her head and pretending to study the dessert menu. Maybe he would walk on by and not see her.

"Afternoon, ladies."

"Hi, Sam," Millicent said with her best smile. She reintroduced Lana, and when their murmured greetings were barely out of their mouths, she added, "Lana and I were just on our way out." Despite Callie's frantic gestures and panicked, silent pleas, her two friends deserted her faster than rats from a sinking ship, and she was left alone with solemn Sam and his censorious frown.

"Your secretary told me where to find you," Sam said. "Mind if I sit down?"

Callie shrugged. She didn't feel like being polite, didn't feel she owed it to him. His coolness from yesterday, and the fact that he doubted her journalistic integrity, still stung.

The moment he settled his tall frame into the booth, the waitress swooped to their table. Sam absently ordered coffee and apple pie, while Callie declined dessert. Her stomach was suddenly tied up in knots.

"Well, go ahead," she said when they were alone. "Tell me everything you hated about my story. Tell me

I'm an opportunistic hack writer. Get it out of your system."

"Callie, I came to apologize. I was way out of line yesterday."

"Yes, you were." She met his steady blue gaze head-on, unwilling to let him off easy. "The *Record* is a responsible newspaper with plenty of readers, thank you. I don't need to entice more with sensationalism."

"So I've been told."

To gain time, Callie pulled off her wire-rim glasses and began cleaning them with a napkin. She didn't know quite what to make of Sam's apology. Was it sincere, or did he have an angle?

"You still wear glasses to make you look older?" he asked. "I figured you'd have gotten over that by now."

"The joke was on me. A couple of years ago I found out I'm nearsighted. These are prescription."

An awkward silence followed. She stirred sugar into her iced tea, not intending to drink it.

"The story on Dad's funeral was good," Sam said abruptly. "It was everything Millicent promised and more. I even liked the picture of Deana, once I saw it."

"Thank you." Callie kept her voice neutral, though she was secretly pleased to know that her agonizing hadn't been for nothing. She'd fluctuated between running Deana's picture or a more generic wide-angle shot of the whole family. She'd finally decided the shot of Deana was in no way offensive or overly melodramatic. The story and picture had run on page three of the Metropolitan section.

"In fact, Mother wants to know if she can get a copy of the photo," Sam continued. "She thought it might be a nice keepsake for Deana, something to remember her grandfather by. I'll pay you." He reached for his wallet.

Callie bristled. "I'll be happy to send you a print, but payment isn't necessary."

"In that case, how about dinner?"

Callie's breath caught in her throat until Sam added, "Mother's doing up a pot roast Thursday night, and she said she'd love to have you."

Callie slowly released her breath. She should have known better than to think, even for an instant, that Sam would ask her out on a date. "I don't want to impose so soon after—"

"She wants you to come. She's been cooking ever since . . . that day, even though the fridge is full of food the neighbors and friends have brought. She says cooking keeps her mind off things."

And a table full of family and guests probably disguised the fact that a certain chair was empty, Callie couldn't help thinking. She had fond memories of all those dinners she'd eaten at the Sangers' house. Johnny had always sat to Sam's immediate right during meals at the small kitchen table. And Sam had always complained—good-naturedly—because his father's elbow was in Sam's face as they ate. It was a standing joke.

Her heart suddenly filled with emotion at the bleak look on Sam's face. He really was grieving, as Millicent had said. Sam had never been one to show his feelings, but in this instant, no matter how hard he tried to keep his sadness hidden, it flowed out of him.

She couldn't seem to say no to him. She had no idea why Beverly Sanger would insist that Callie come to dinner, but she didn't think it had been Sam's idea.

"Will it bother you if I come?" she asked. "If you'd rather I stay away—"

"I'd like you to come. It's the least I can do to make up for the things I said yesterday."

"Then I'll come. Can I bring anything besides the picture?"

He shook his head. "Mother's always been real fond of you. I'm sure just having you around will be like a tonic for her."

Sam's pie arrived. He took a couple of bites without comment. Then, despite the fact that the Pie Pantry served the best homemade desserts in the county, he pushed his plate aside and scooted out of the booth.

"See you Thursday, around seven." He donned his beige felt Stetson, pulled some money out of his jeans pocket, laid it on the table, and left without further comment.

Callie watched him go, admiring the fit of worn denim on his backside despite herself. He'd filled out some since she'd last seen him, exchanging his thin, wiry build for one that was still lean but well muscled.

"Lean and mean," she murmured, knowing the phrase wasn't accurate. Sam wasn't the least bit mean, but he did know what he wanted out of life and he usually got it.

She could only hope he never decided he wanted her again. As teenagers they'd done their share of kissing and caressing, sometimes with their clothes more off than on. But Callie had been afraid to consummate their mutual desire. She'd thought they were too young, their future too uncertain. She'd worried about everything from her "reputation" to unplanned pregnancies. Sam, though he'd been burning to make love to her, had respected her wishes.

But she'd always wondered.

As an adult woman, she wasn't sure she would have the same qualms she'd had eight years ago. That was one temptation she hoped she never had to face.

TWO

Callie turned down the Sangers' street, her chest tight with anticipation. The neighborhood looked the same as always—fences in need of mending, fields either overgrown or overgrazed, potholes galore. There was just something about this pocket of land that wasn't conducive to farming, yet the owners here hung on, many of them for generations.

The Sangers had one of the nicest farms in the area, though that wasn't saying much. But at least the fences were standing and the big frame house looked as if someone had painted it in recent memory. Johnny Sanger might not have earned a fortune in his life, but what little he'd had, he'd taken care of. The front yard was neatly landscaped, with hardly a single fall leaf to mar the still-green grass. He must have worked daily on the yard right up until his death.

Callie parked her car between a rented sedan—Sam's, no doubt—and a disreputable-looking brown pickup. A dog's barking greeted her as she rang the bell.

Callie was surprised to hear a dog inside the house. Johnny Sanger had never allowed dogs inside—another symptom of his fastidiousness.

Beverly opened the door and greeted Callie with a brittle smile. "Come in, sweetie, come in. Here, let me take that—oh, for us?" She indicated a basket Callie held, heaped high with pecans and tied with a red bow.

"I thought you could freeze them until you're ready to do your next round of baking." Callie also held an envelope containing her photo of Deana, which she placed on a table in the entry hall. The dog, a collie, put her nose into the basket, and Callie petted her then shooed her away.

Beverly closed the door and took Callie's jacket, hanging it on a hook inside the coat closet. "Oh, heavens, the baking never ends around here. Come in, come in, and let's have a visit while we're still alone. Sam's out tending the chickens." They settled onto the couch, and Beverly cleared her throat nervously. "I've been meaning to talk to you about something. I tried to discuss it with Sam, but he shut me up real quick. Doesn't want to hear a word."

"What is it, Bev?"

"It's about Johnny. About the police's ruling on his death. I'm having a very hard time with it."

"Well, that's only natural. No one wants to believe their husband—"

"It's not just that I can't accept it. I flat out don't believe it."

Callie's skin prickled. "Why's that?"

Beverly glanced from side to side, as if she was making sure no one would overhear. "I feel like I'm being objective now, not emotional," she assured Callie. "You know I found Johnny in his office. The place looked like a tornado had hit it. I simply can't believe Johnny would leave his office that way, I don't care how much he'd been drinking or how despondent he was."

Callie reluctantly nodded. "I saw the police photos. I was surprised at the mess too. But we can't really know what was going through his head."

"They say he did it for the life insurance, because we had so many debts, and by dying, he'd be sure I was set for life. That's even harder to believe."

"But the policy was found sitting out on the desk," Callie reasoned, recalling the police report. "He must have taken it out and read it that day for a reason."

"But why? Why that day? It doesn't make any sense. The farm was doing fine this year—so well, in fact, that we tore up the check Sam sent us. He usually helps us out once or twice a year, whenever he has some spare cash. But for the first time we didn't need it. So this business of Johnny being all upset because we were broke is nonsense."

"Maybe there was another reason," Callie said. "He could have been upset about something else."

"But what?"

"Health problems?" Callie suggested.

"They did an autopsy. He was fit as a fiddle. And we weren't having marital problems, either. Oh, the police asked me that first thing. Not that we had a perfect marriage, but who does?"

Callie was at a loss. "You know, Beverly, if it wasn't suicide, the alternative isn't any more pleasant."

Beverly nodded grimly. "I know. I guess it's not very likely that a stranger broke in, murdered Johnny, and faked his suicide."

"Possible, but not likely," Callie agreed. She knew the statistics. Most murders were committed by people known to the victims.

Suddenly Beverly looked at Callie with desperate eyes. "I have to know, Callie. I have to know if my son, my flesh and blood, is a murderer." She covered her face. "I'm so ashamed that the thought even crosses my mind. But with Will's history and all . . ."

Callie laid a hand on Bev's shoulder. The possibility had nibbled at the edges of her mind too. Will Sanger's arrest record was impressive, though he'd never shown a penchant for violent crime.

"The police won't listen to me," Beverly said with a sigh. "They just think I'm a hysterical woman who can't accept the obvious."

"Maybe you should try again."

Beverly shook her head emphatically. "No. Not unless I have something more to tell them than just my gut feelings. And it wouldn't be fair to Will to accuse him without more evidence."

Uh-oh. Callie had a feeling she knew what was coming next. Beverly's dinner invitation suddenly made more sense. "Beverly, I hope you don't want me to—"

"But you're so good at it! I've been reading your stories in the newspaper for years now. You know how to get to the heart of any crime—not just because you see and record the facts, but because you can read people. You know what makes them tick. And I know you've worked with the police in the past."

Callie sighed and nodded. She couldn't seem to say no to her friend. "I'll keep my eyes and ears open. If I find out anything helpful to you, I'll tell you."

"Oh, thank you, dear. You don't know what it means to me." Beverly's focus shifted to the basket of pecans. "Are these from your mom's trees?"

Callie nodded as they both stood up, as if in unspoken agreement that official business was finished, and headed for the kitchen. "New crop. Gathered this morning."

"How thoughtful of you, Callie. Those trees always produced the sweetest nuts in the county. My Johnny just loves—loved—" Beverly faltered, halting midstep.

"It's okay, Beverly. You don't have to pretend or be brave in front of me."

"My lands, who will eat my pecan pie?" Beverly said on a sob. "It was his favorite. Neither of my boys care for it much."

"Then make pecan shortbread cookies instead." Callie felt woefully inadequate for this task. She remembered when she'd lost her own father, and how she'd felt powerless to help her mother through the ordeal. She felt the same sense of helplessness now. Still, she tried. "You can always donate your extra pies and things to the Lions Club bake sale." Inwardly, Callie winced. Why had she thought pecans were such an inspired gift?

The collie shifted from one paw to another, looking up anxiously at her mistress.

Beverly sniffled loudly as she searched her apron pockets for a tissue. "Why, that's a wonderful idea.

Johnny would like for his pies to go to a worthy cause. He was always thinking of other people. That's why I just can't understand—" This time she broke down completely.

Callie, feeling a bit panicky, put her arm around Beverly's frail shoulders. "It'll be okay, Bev. I know it hurts so much now—" But Callie didn't know. She'd never lost a spouse. The only thing that had come close was when she'd learned that Sam had married and she'd realized he was out of her reach forever. She'd cried every night for two weeks. How much more horrible it must be to lose your husband to a senseless act of violence.

Sam chose that moment to enter the living room. He took one look at his grief-stricken mother, then cast a faintly accusing look at Callie. "Mom?"

Callie stepped out of the way so that Sam could offer his own comfort. She shouldn't have come. She was just upsetting things.

"It's okay, Mom," Sam crooned. "Don't cry. It'll be okay."

Callie felt tears of frustration pressing at the back of her eyes, caused not only by Beverly's distress, but by the unspoken censure reflected in Sam's expression. "I brought pecans," she confessed. "I didn't realize pecan pie was Johnny's favorite."

Beverly rapidly pulled herself together. "Oh, Callie, you didn't do anything wrong." The sentence was punctuated by a hiccup. "It was a very thoughtful gift, and I love that you took the time to put together something from your family, from your heart. But Sam can tell you, the least little thing sets me off."

"I guess we're all a little raw," Sam mumbled. "It's easy to overreact. Sorry."

Callie nodded her acceptance of the grudging apology, wishing that she could stop rubbing him the wrong way. But then, she hadn't come here to curry favor with Sam. She wanted to help, to somehow ease the hurt that had been inflicted on this already troubled family. Seeing the haunted look in his eyes, she didn't believe she could possibly succeed.

"I'll just, um, put these somewhere." She started to ease her way toward the kitchen door.

Beverly halted her by touching her shoulder. "No, give them to Sam." She dried the last of her tears with the corner of her apron and looked up at her son. "You might as well start shelling these. I'll get working on those pies right away. There's a bake sale at the Baptist church next weekend. Won't they be surprised to get a donated pie from a Methodist?" She tittered at her own joke, then nudged Callie toward the kitchen. "You don't mind keeping me company while I work on dinner, do you?"

"No, and I'd love to help, if you have something a kitchen klutz can handle." She gave a backward glance at Sam, realizing as she did that she was hungry for the sight of him. She wished she could linger in the living room a few more minutes, just to drink in that sun-streaked hair and bronzed skin, the broad shoulders, the slim, cowboy's hips encased in jeans.

He gazed back at her, holding the basket of pecans like it was some object from another planet, a perplexed look on his face. And something else. Was that a flicker of desire she'd seen in his eyes? Some vestige of the fire that had once burned between them like a white-hot blowtorch?

Don't be ridiculous, she thought with a shake of her head as she moved into the kitchen with Beverly.

The kitchen smelled wonderful, like the blend of a hundred mouthwatering fragrances from countless years of home cooking. "Mmm, what's on the menu?" she asked. "Sam said something about pot roast?" To her discomfort, Sam followed them into the kitchen. He grabbed a nutcracker from a drawer, sat down at the roomy kitchen table, and began shelling the pecans without comment.

"Changed my mind," Beverly replied. "Now it's roast chicken and mashed potatoes, and some green beans I canned this summer."

"Sounds like heaven to me. Ever since I've been living on my own, all I have time for is frozen stuff and fast food."

"Well, I expect that's normal for a career girl like yourself."

Callie had to struggle to keep from looking at Sam. Her "career" had always been a sore subject between them. When she'd refused to drop everything and move to Nevada with him, he'd accused her of putting fame and fortune and professional aims ahead of love and personal goals. And maybe she had. But so had he. He hadn't been willing to give up his precious ranch for her.

Granted, a fifty-thousand-acre cattle spread was a little different than an internship at a small-town daily newspaper. Round Rock was more of a family legacy. But she figured it wasn't the size of the professional goal that mattered, it was the principle of the thing. He'd acted as if her job, her aspirations, were insignificant fluff.

"I can do that," Callie volunteered when Beverly began scrubbing potatoes.

"Exactly what I had in mind. The peeler is in that top drawer over there, beside the oven. I figure even the worst kind of kitchen klutz can peel potatoes. Sam, if you're going to hang around in the kitchen, why don't you help peel."

"I thought you wanted me to shell pecans," he said gruffly.

"Whatever you prefer," Beverly responded mildly. "Although if the only thing you're going to contribute to the conversation is scowls and throat clearing, I'd just as soon you went somewhere else."

Callie tensed, and for a moment it felt like her heart had stopped beating. She loved Beverly, but she wished the older woman wouldn't push the matter. She didn't want to be a source of conflict between Sam and his mother.

"I wasn't aware that I was scowling." Sam looked straight at Callie. "But if I'm making anyone uncomfortable, I'll leave."

"I'm not uncomfortable," Callie blurted out, then could have bitten out her own tongue. She wanted him to leave! she told herself. "Please, Sam, stay. I can handle the potatoes if you'll do the pecans. I'm looking forward to that pecan pie."

"Well, at least someone is," Beverly said, a mischievous smile lifting one corner of her mouth. "So, Callie, what's been going on at the paper these days?"

Callie relaxed a bit, glad for something neutral to talk about. She engaged in small talk with Beverly for a few minutes as they all worked at their assigned tasks. The smell of herbs wafted across the kitchen, bringing with it the memory of many long-ago evenings just like this, when she and Sam would be hanging out in the kitchen, snapping peas or beating meringue for that night's pie, sharing stories of their days. If she closed her eyes, she could imagine Sam's easygoing smile. The one she hadn't seen in years.

"Where's Deana?" she suddenly thought to ask.

"She's with Millicent Jones," Beverly answered when it became obvious Sam wasn't going to. "Her youngest is about Deana's age. Millicent offered to take them both to that new Kid-Gym place where they have the tunnels and rooms full of balloons and stuff."

"Oh, yeah, that place that looks like a HabiTrail for humans?" Callie looked directly at Sam, making an honest attempt to connect with him on some level. She didn't see any reason why they should be awkward around each other for the rest of their lives. Not that she'd be seeing him much, she reminded herself, but on those rare occasions when they did cross paths, it would be nice if they could get along—for Beverly's sake if nothing else.

"It's not my idea of a load of fun," Sam said. "But Millicent claims she tags right along with the kids, crawling around on hands and knees, swinging on ropes, climbing ladders. I don't think my knees could take it."

Callie was gratified that at least she'd gotten a snippet of normal conversation from Sam. "I can see Millicent crawling through those tunnels with the kids." For a moment Callie felt a stab of jealousy for her friend, who was so happy and relaxed around children—her own three, or umpteen from her neighborhood who trailed in and out of her house. Right now Deana was probably bonding with Millicent. . . . Now why in the world would that idea be so bothersome? Callie had no desire for any child to "bond" with her, particularly not Sam's. She'd made her decision years ago to forgo, or at least postpone, having a family until her career was well established.

That hadn't happened yet. Oh, sure, she was editor of the paper. But that was in Destiny, Texas, where hardly anything happened. She wanted a chance at the big time—*The Washington Post. The New York Times.* Or at least the *Houston Chronicle.* Only a couple of weeks ago she'd sent out a new batch of résumés, a ritual she went through once a year.

She forced her attention back to the present. At least she and Sam were talking, sort of.

"Oh, darn," Beverly said, "I'm out of, uh, sage for the chicken."

"I think we'll survive without it," Sam said dryly.

"No, no, this recipe just isn't the same without sage. I'll run next door and borrow some from Rebecca Keyes."

"Rebecca's is half a mile away."

"No problem."

"I could go get it—" Callie tried.

"No, I need the walk," Beverly insisted. "You two hold down the fort."

Well, that was subtle, Callie thought as she tried and failed to come up with some sort of reasonable objection to being left alone with Sam. If she didn't know better . . . ah, hell, she did know better. Beverly had left them alone on purpose, hoping they would mend some fences.

Callie cleared her throat. "Um, how're things at the ranch?"

"Are you asking to be polite, or do you really want to know?"

Although her blood was threatening to boil, she put a lid on it. If Sam was spoiling for a fight, he wasn't going to get one from her. "Both," she said with what she hoped resembled a pleasant smile. "I'm interested in your welfare, which means I'd like to know how your life's work is going. And I think it would be nice if we could be civil to one another, so I'm making an effort."

"My, haven't you learned to be diplomatic over the years."

"It helps in my profession not to provoke people. They seldom are cooperative during an interview if you make them angry."

"And do I make you angry?"

Enough that she felt like flinging her bowl of potato peelings at him. "Yes. I don't understand why you can't be a bit more pleasant. It couldn't be because you're still smarting over our breakup all those years ago. Could it?"

She held her breath. Good Lord, what had made her say that? By baiting him, she was behaving as childishly as he.

"I'm not the one carrying a flame. I got on with my life. I married, had a family. You're the one holding out."

"Well, I . . . How could you—" Oh, if he only knew how close he was to wearing those potato peels. "You turkey!"

A low laugh rumbled from Sam's throat, sounding rusty. "Is that the best you can do?"

Okay, so as epithets went, *turkey* was pretty weak. "Years ago I'd have called you much worse," she said primly, "but I'd like to think I've matured a little since those days. Besides," she added, "I am a guest in your home."

His amusement only increased, which further infuriated her. "Yes, you are," he agreed with exaggerated formality. "I guess I've overstepped the bounds of politeness."

Callie snorted. "Like the bounds of politeness ever restricted you before."

His eyes crackled with blue fire. "You're really cruisin' for a bruisin'."

"Oh, yeah?"

"Yup, I think someone needs to teach you a lesson."

"You and who else? You never could get the best of me, even when we were kids."

"That's because my mother wouldn't let me roughhouse with girls, even when they hit me first. She still won't, for that matter."

"Then how're you going to teach me a lesson?" Callie laughed suddenly, then bit her lip. She couldn't believe she had stooped to this juvenile war of words with Sam, not when she knew how it had always ended before. He would get that look in his eye, and then he would chase her until she let him catch her and throw her over his shoulder, fireman style. Then he would carry her to the nearest sofa, drop her onto it, and proceed to tickle her into submission. Or kiss her.

As she recalled, it was just such a confrontation that had led to their first kiss.

The way Sam was looking at her, she was willing to bet his thoughts were running along the same lines. He slowly set the nutcracker aside. His chair rumbled backward as he stood.

He licked his lips. She swallowed.

Oh, dear, she'd carried this thing too far. "I only meant to loosen things up between us, Sam." She took an instinctive half step backward. "I hate it that you're so . . . cold toward me. I just want us to be friends again."

He shook his head as if to clear it of fog. "I'm not sure that's possible. We haven't been 'just friends' since we hit puberty."

"We can try," she insisted, although she partly agreed with him. They'd liked each other as children—had played on the same Little League team, gone to church camp together. In seventh grade they'd despised each other—or, perhaps facing an attraction they didn't yet understand, they'd only pretended the intense dislike. At some point during eighth grade their seething hormones had won out, and they'd become inseparable. And, as Sam had said, from that point on they'd never again been simply friends. They'd either been madly in love or broken up and furious with each other until they made up.

Callie held out her hand. "C'mon, Sam. Friends? Can we let bygones be bygones?"

He never verbally agreed to her terms, but he did

take her hand. Instead of the perfunctory shake she'd expected, he held her palm against his, testing its softness with his strength. A million fireflies fluttered up her arm, then spread their flickering warmth throughout her body, settling deep in her abdomen where her most womanly urges resided.

The doorbell rang. In a moment of irrational panic, Callie tried to jerk her hand from Sam's grasp. He held on to her, daring her to make an issue of it. When the front door opened, however, and a cheery voice called in, "Yoo-hoo, anyone home?" Sam finally abandoned the game.

"In here, Millicent," he called over his shoulder.

A whirling dervish, two feet high and wearing a grass-green jacket, burst through the kitchen doorway. "Daddy!"

Sam scooped his daughter into his arms. "Hi, Deany! Did you have fun with Mrs. Jones and Lily?"

Deana immediately launched into a long monologue about her afternoon's adventures that no doubt made perfect sense to her. Callie, however, caught only about every fifth word.

Sam seemed to understand. "A dinosaur's mouth? And then what happened? Did the dinosaur try to eat you?"

"Nooo!" She laughed uproariously, her blue eyes sparkling. But it wasn't her smile that brought a lump to Callie's throat, it was Sam's. In the split second it had taken for him to greet his daughter, his whole demeanor had changed. He was smiling, animated. Love poured out of him like a bright beam of light enveloping Deana. Even his posture had changed. Instead of looking like he had a fire poker up his back, he was in a relaxed, easy stance.

Memories danced inside Callie's head, memories of when Sam had looked at her with love in his eyes. She suddenly ached all over to have him look at her that way again.

Millicent leaned into the kitchen doorway. "Oh, hi, Callie. I thought I recognized that car out front."

Callie almost laughed. Millicent had known good and well that Callie was joining the Sangers for dinner that night. They'd talked about it at least three times on the phone earlier this week.

"Hi, Millie."

"Can you stay for dinner?" Sam asked. "There's plenty of food."

"No, I've got a car full of kids with me, and Nancy has to get to her viola lesson. But thanks. Is your mom here?"

Sam shook his head. "Went to borrow some spices from the neighbor."

"Oh. I was going to ask her for a couple dozen eggs. But I can come back—"

"No, no problem, I'll get them." Sam set Deana on the ground and went to the huge double-sided refrigerator. "Yeah, looks like she's got plenty. I don't know what she charges for them, though."

"I do. I have the exact change right here."

During Sam and Millicent's exchange, Deana had wandered over to Callie's side. Feeling awkward, Callie leaned down to attempt a conversation. "Hi, Deana. I'm Callie."

"Cal? Dem soxis poody."

"What?"

Millicent laughed. "She's saying your stockings are pretty." She indicated Callie's lace-textured hose.

"Oh. Uh, thank you. Your, uh, barrette is pretty too." Callie touched it lightly, pondering the purple cartoon character. "Is that a . . . a hippopotamus?"

Deana looked horrified. "Iss Barney!"

Millicent laughed again. "Get with it, Callie."

"Oops. Oh, yes, now I see. Of course it's Barney. Guess I need new glasses."

Sam returned, carrying two cardboard cartons of eggs.

Millicent laid a couple of bills and some change on the table and took the eggs. "Thanks."

"Sure you won't stay for dinner?"

"Can't. Nancy would have a fit if she missed her viola class. But it's nice of you to ask. Another time, maybe. Oh, we had a little accident." She handed Sam a diaper bag.

"No problem," Sam said easily. "We have lots of little accidents, don't we, Deana? But we're working on it."

"My Lily is still in diapers, so don't feel too badly."

"I won't." He smiled warmly at her. "Thanks, Millicent."

"No problem. See ya, Callie. Bye, Deana."

"Bye bye!" Deana waved her chubby hand at Millicent as the latter disappeared.

"Potty training, huh?" Callie said, feeling really ignorant.

"Yup. Speaking of the P-word," Sam said, "Deana, do you need to use the bathroom?"

"Mmm, don't know," she said cheerfully.

"Okay, well, maybe we better give it a try. Excuse us, Callie."

"Yeah, 'scoose us." Deana giggled, touching Callie's heart with her ingenuousness, before leaving the room with her father.

"I don't hafta go, Daddy," Deana said.

"Well, that's okay if you don't, but just sit there for a couple of minutes to be sure, okay?"

"Mmm, okay."

And give Daddy a few minutes of peace away from Callie Calloway, he added silently. Damn, he'd forgotten what that girl—woman, he should say—could do to him. He considered himself a controlled man, one who didn't easily give in to emotion. He had accepted his wife's desertion with his usual stoicism, having realized early in the marriage that it wasn't going to work. Debra's unexpected pregnancy had kept things together for a while, but even Deana couldn't preserve her parents' marriage indefinitely, not when there was no love left between them—if there had ever been any to begin with.

Even his father's suicide Sam had taken with outward pragmatism, if not inner acceptance. He and Johnny Sanger hadn't exactly seen eye to eye on much of anything, but Sam had respected his old man for sticking with the firm against the worst odds, and for his continued loyalty to Beverly. His abrupt departure from this world had hurt, no doubt about it, and Sam would have to deal with the pain eventually, but he hadn't lost control.

Now, along comes his childhood sweetheart, a slip of a girl with whom he'd shared an on-again, off-again, essentially immature relationship, one who had practically stomped on his heart with her refusal to marry him, and he was as stoic as Silly Putty, as controlled as a stampeding herd of cattle.

He never should have looked into those earnest brown eyes, much less have touched her. One glance, one almost caress, and he'd been thrown back eight years. He'd thought his adolescent adoration of Callie had long since been dealt with and buried. But it appeared he was wrong.

"Done, Daddy," Deana said proudly.

"Well, I'll be darned," Sam said. "I knew you could do it! See, this toilet-training stuff is a breeze, isn't it?"

"Bweeze," Deana experimented. She liked the sound of the word, so she said it over and over.

As Sam helped Deana wash her hands he decided that this dinner with Callie was simply something to be endured. She was right about one thing, though. He should behave civilly toward her. Their breakup was ancient history, and it would be silly of him to hold a grudge. She'd done nothing recently to justify treating her with anything but respect and politeness—unless she was intent on stirring up trouble about his father's death, and so far that didn't seem to be the case.

"So that's what I'll do," he told his reflection in the mirror. "I'll be polite, I'll be pleasant." No more silly conversation burgeoning with sexual innuendo. No more smart comebacks or attempts at one-upmanship.

He would treat her with friendliness, but impersonally—the way he did Millicent Jones, for example.

Once he proved, to both himself and Callie, that the feelings he harbored were nothing but a fond remembrance of a childhood sweetheart, they could move on.

If he could just get through dinner without saying something stupid . . . and then what?

Well, he wasn't staying in Destiny very long, anyway—just long enough to help his mother push the will through probate, collect Dad's life insurance, straighten out the bills, and get the farm business back on track where she could manage it. A few weeks at the most.

If he ran into Callie during that time, he would be prepared. He would handle it.

But he'd give anything to be back on his ranch, in the saddle, cutting through a keen wind, with nothing more pressing on his mind than rounding up a few strays.

THREE

Sam washed his own hands and ran a comb through his hair. "Okay, I think we're—Deana?"

Apparently, during his lengthy soul-searching, she'd wandered out of the bathroom. Feeling a pinprick of panic, even though he knew she couldn't wander far, he went in search of her. She wasn't hard to find. She was in the kitchen, sitting on Callie's lap.

"Looky, Daddy!" she exclaimed the moment she caught sight of her father. She held up a fuzzy yellow toy that appeared to be a baby chick. "Cal gimme."

"Oh, very nice." Sam bit his tongue. But if he bit it any harder, he would bleed. So to Callie he added, "That was thoughtful of you. But I thought you didn't like kids."

Callie's jaw dropped open for an instant, but then she quickly composed herself. "I never said I didn't like kids. I don't know much about them, but I still like them."

"Think you'll ever have any of your own?" All right,

so he was being nosy. Callie's interest in Deana, though nothing to be shocked about, intrigued him.

"I don't know. But I have a few more years to decide. Heck, I might not even get married."

"A few years ago marriage didn't appeal to you, but I thought maybe your biological clock had kicked in by now."

"Not even a little," she said flatly, though the way she cuddled Deana—and the way Deana responded—made him wonder about her self-avowed lack of maternal instincts. "Sam, surely you don't think that because I brought your daughter a present, I have my sights set on a ready-made family?"

"Of course not. I'm just making conversation."

"You're deliberately provoking me."

Okay, so maybe he was. Maybe he'd never gotten over the fact that she'd chosen her career over him. It was his damned male pride, that was all. He didn't really want Callie. She was way too bristly, too stubborn, and too independent to make a good wife and mother. But she brought out this belligerent streak in him that he couldn't seem to control.

Callie's face went neutral. She gently set a protesting Deana on the floor. "I wanted to be friends with you, Sam, but apparently that's not possible. I'm not sure if you have a chip on your shoulder, or if you just enjoy making me uncomfortable. Either way, I can't deal with it anymore. So I'll be on my way." She paused, then awkwardly patted Deana on the head. "Good-bye, Deana."

"Wait!" Sam called after her as she exited the kitchen by punching through the swinging door like a fist. He followed her to the front of the house. "You're not staying for dinner?"

"It's too uncomfortable for me, Sam. Your mother doesn't need to deal with the tension between us. You know how she is. She'll assume the role of peacemaker. She has more important things to deal with right now." Callie found her jacket and jabbed her arms through the sleeves.

"What am I supposed to tell my mother?"

"How about the truth? That you needled me until you drove me away."

"I can't tell her that!"

Callie sighed. "Then make something up."

"Wait, wait, Callie—" He grabbed her by the arm and spun her around.

She looked up at him expectantly, her brown eyes aglow with the molten lava of repressed emotions. "Wait? For what?"

Sam couldn't think of anything to keep her there, not one damn thing, except . . . Before he could stop himself he'd leaned down and captured her mouth with his. And for one split second, one tiny sliver of remembered heaven, she kissed him back.

Then, apparently, she came to her senses. She pushed him away and raised her hand as if to slap him. He was so sure she was going to do it that he braced himself for the blow, knowing he deserved that and more.

But slowly she lowered her arm as she stared up at him, chest heaving, bottom lip trembling. "You are so incredibly juvenile."

"I am?"

"Once upon a time that might have worked. You could kiss me and I'd forgive anything. But I'm not that easy anymore, Sam Sanger." She stepped back, still staring. Abruptly she turned and fled.

Sam shook his head. So much for control.

Callie managed not to lose control until she was safely in her car and off Sanger property. Then she pulled off the road and shook for a full five minutes.

What had Sam been trying to prove with that stupid kiss—that he still had some hold on her?

Unfortunately, that was exactly what he'd proved—to her, anyway. Until then she'd been fine, everything under tight rein. But one touch of his mouth to hers and she'd become a lump of sugar melting in a thunderstorm. Everything she'd pushed aside over the years—the memories of loving, laughing, battling, and wanting—had risen from some previously uncharted region of her brain to engulf her.

It had taken every ounce of willpower she'd had and then some to pull away, to deny the sexual pull he'd reawakened with that one simple, complicated kiss. She still wasn't sure how she'd done it, how she'd spoken coherently, or why her wobbly legs hadn't dumped her unceremoniously onto the floor.

After a few more minutes she felt okay enough to drive. But her lips still tingled, and the memory of Sam's embrace, the strength of his hands as he grasped her arms, the smell of his aftershave, stayed with her.

Since she'd done herself out of dinner, and she knew darn well her freezer was empty, she had to find something to eat. She was thinking about Mexi-Taco when she stopped to fill up her car. Then she spied some frozen burritos in the case at the mini-mart where she bought her gas and decided that would fill her stomach as well as anything.

As she stood in line to pay for her purchases, she recognized the cop in front of her—Sloan Bennett, who'd graduated from high school with her. He'd been the black sheep of the class, the motorcycle-riding bad boy who was always getting into fights. The one all of her friends' mothers warned them to stay away from.

And he'd become a cop, of all things.

"Hey, Sloan," she said when he'd finished paying for his gas. They hadn't known each other at all in high school, but they'd become acquainted in the course of their respective jobs.

"Oh, hi, Callie. That your dinner?" he asked, raising a skeptical eyebrow.

"Uh-huh."

"That's kind of pitiful. I was just heading over to Sal's for some lasagna. You can tag along if you like."

She started to refuse. She wanted nothing more than to run home and hibernate. The idea of going someplace public where she had to maintain a facade that everything was peachy . . . On the other hand, Sloan was someone she'd been meaning to talk to. The police report on Johnny Sanger's death had mentioned Sloan as one of the first officers on the scene. But he'd been unavailable for an interview, and she'd had a deadline.

"C'mon, put those disgusting things back in the case," he said.

"Hey," the clerk, Alma Potter, objected. "You want

to insult the food I sell, you can buy your coffee and doughnuts somewhere else."

Sloan laughed. "Okay, you win. They're not disgusting. But Callie could do better."

"Hmmph," Alma said.

"All right, I'll go with you to Sal's." Callie paid for her gas, returned the burritos to their case, and followed Sloan the two blocks down Main Street to Sal's Pizzeria.

Maybe someone would see them having dinner together and Sam would hear about it, she thought smugly. At any rate, it couldn't do her reputation any harm to be seen with Sloan. With his curly black hair and a college quarterback's body, he was handsome as sin and always the object of speculation among the women she knew.

She and Sloan found an empty booth in a dimly lit corner.

"You were one of the first to arrive at the scene when Johnny Sanger died, right?" Callie asked after she'd made the requisite small talk.

Immediately a wary look came into Sloan's eyes. "Are you asking as a reporter, or as a friend?"

"Mmm, a little of both. I mean, the story's done, and I don't have any firm plans to write anything else about it. But I'd wanted to talk to you. Just to kind of tie up the loose ends."

"You know I can't do any official interviews without approval from the department."

"Yeah, I guess I knew that," she reluctantly admitted. "Tell you what. Just talk to me, off the record. If for any reason I should want to use what you've told me, I'll go back and get permission. Fair?"

"Sure, no problem."

Callie had worked hard to earn trust from the police department and various other civic authorities over the years. She'd gained a reputation as a straight shooter. If she told someone their words were off the record, she meant it. Consequently, her sources were open with her. The police in particular were always cooperative. More than once she'd offered up information she'd gleaned from researching a story that had helped them out.

"What exactly is it you want to know?"

"What was the scene like when you got there?" she asked. "I mean, I saw the police photos, but sometimes those two-dimensional pictures don't do a scene justice. What were your personal impressions?"

"You sure you want to talk about this while we're eating?"

"I'm tough," she said with a smile. And she meant it. She'd seen enough crime-scene photos over the years, and a few scenes up close and personal, that she could detach herself when necessary.

"Well, Jerry Langly and I got the call. Mrs. Sanger let us in. She was pretty cool under the circumstances; in shock, I'd guess. She showed us where the study was. Said she and her daughter-in-law had just come home from grocery shopping and found him. Neither of them stayed long in the room, and she didn't believe they touched anything. They just turned, walked out, and Mrs. Sanger dialed nine-one-one. Then they called in the older son, Tamra's husband. . . ."

"Will," Callie provided.

"Right. He'd been out in the fields plowing or something. Some neighbors verified that."

"So Johnny was in his office? And he was already dead?"

"Real dead, I'm afraid." Sloan went on to describe where exactly Johnny had been lying, where the two loads of shot had entered his body—first in his solar plexus, then the fatal wound in his chest—how he was holding the gun. The details were a bit gruesome, but Callie just kept eating her lasagna, wanting Sloan to continue.

When he paused, she prompted him with a question that had been bothering her. "Isn't it a little unusual for a suicide to shoot himself twice?"

"A little, not unheard of. The first shot doesn't always do the trick."

Callie nodded. "Okay, now with this type of murder—"

"Don't you mean suicide?"

That brought her up short. Why had she said murder? "Oh, of course I mean suicide. I don't know what I was thinking."

"Callie, is there some reason you suspect foul play?"

She sighed. "I don't know. Something just doesn't feel right. I got the impression that the police were eager to close the case—not for any nefarious reason," she added hastily when Sloan started to object, "but because everyone remembers the hell that family went through with the drunk-driving scandal years ago, and no one wants to cause Beverly any more heartache than is necessary."

"So you think something might have been over-looked in their haste?" Sloan asked skeptically.

"Not anything obvious. The bases were covered. The wounds were from almost point-blank range, there was gunpowder residue on Johnny's right hand, significant amounts of alcohol in his system—all consistent with suicide."

"But . . . ?"

She shrugged helplessly. "Can't put my finger on it. I do feel it's odd he didn't leave a note."

"A lot of them don't, especially if it's a spur-of-the-moment decision. I mean, picture this: He was drinking, looking over the finances, feeling despair because he never amounted to much, overwhelmed by the continual debt. He searched through his files for some kind of salvation. He finds the insurance policy. The gun was handy . . . *pow*. He ends it all."

Callie gave an involuntary shiver. She wasn't as tough as she thought. "That just doesn't seem consistent with the Johnny Sanger I knew. I can't believe he would do that to Beverly—shoot himself, knowing she would find his body. And from what Beverly says, their finances weren't in that bad a shape."

"Danny Fowler said their debt was pretty staggering."

"Danny—oh." The detective who investigated the Sanger death. "I'll bet if he checked, he'd discover the debt has been much worse in past years."

Sloan took a tiny notebook out of his breast pocket and made a note. "It's worth a second thought." He looked at his watch. "I need to get back on patrol. Any more questions?"

Callie thought hard. "Were you aware that Johnny Sanger was something of a neatness freak?"

"Couldn't have told that from looking at his office."

Callie nodded. Sloan had made her point for her. "By the way, the last thing I want is to cause the police to harangue Beverly with any more painful questions—unless there's a really good reason."

"Like murder?"

The phone rang, waking Callie out of an uneasy sleep. She glanced at the illuminated dial of her bedside clock before answering. It was after two.

"Hello?" she said muzzily.

"Callie? It's Sam."

Sam? "Is something wrong?" Her heart went into overdrive.

"Hell, yeah, something's wrong. I can't sleep."

She fell limply against her pillow. "That's it? You can't sleep? You woke me up at two in the morning to tell me that?" If the truth be known, Callie'd had a hard time falling asleep herself. Between memories of Sam's kiss and her suspicions about Johnny's death, her mind had been awhirl with questions that had no easy answers.

"You're the reason I have insomnia."

"I should have known you'd find a way to blame me," she said dryly, stacking two pillows together and propping her head on them. She was awake now, so she might as well give this conversation her best.

"I blame me. I let you get to me."

"But I didn't do anything!" she protested.

"I'm not saying you did anything wrong. You just get under my skin, Callie."

She made no reply to that.

"Okay, I know what you're waiting for. I'm sorry if my less-than-sterling behavior drove you away. Geez, this must be some kind of record, three apologies in one week."

"Maybe if you'd stop acting like a horse's behind, you wouldn't have to apologize so often."

"Guess I had that coming."

"Yup. Sam," she said, abandoning their verbal sparring, "you do understand why I came to dinner, don't you?"

"Because I asked you?"

"Because your mother wanted me to come." It was a lie of omission only. She had gone to the Sangers' last night because of Beverly, but also because she found it nearly impossible to say no to Sam, especially when he was being humble and earnest. "Difficult as it may be for you to understand this, Beverly and I are friends. You know I've enjoyed being around her ever since I was a kid, and we remained close even after you and I broke up. I didn't want to avoid seeing her, especially at a time when she most needs her friends, just because you happen to be in town."

"Very noble of you," Sam said. "Are you telling me you weren't just the least bit curious to see how I'd changed during the last eight years? Curious about my daughter? Curious to know if those ol' embers were still glowing beneath all the ashes?"

Callie took a deep breath. "You're doing it again."

"Doing what?"

She rolled her eyes. The man was hopeless. He was also a little too perceptive for her own comfort. "Maybe I was curious," she admitted. "But I've got my answer now, haven't I? You're as bullheaded as ever, just as determined to be right, to be in charge. You've only confirmed that I made the right decision eight years ago."

She thought she heard a whoosh of air coming from Sam, but through the telephone lines it was hard to tell. Good, she thought. He needed to have the wind taken out of his sails once in a while.

"And that kiss meant nothing to you?" he said after a long pause.

Damn, he was pulling out the heavy artillery. The kiss! Just the memory of it made her stomach do cartwheels and her thighs tingle. "Of course it meant nothing," she bluffed.

His silence was quite obviously a sign of skepticism.

"It brought back a certain nostalgia," she said, "but that's all. It meant nothing in terms of the present or the future."

"Then why did I detect a response?" he asked in that soft, sexy voice that sent shivers down her spine.

"Because you were hallucinating?" she shot back.

He answered with a low chuckle.

"Well, for heaven's sake, I'm allowed to have hormones. Maybe one or two got in the way for a moment, but in the grand scheme of things, hormonal reactions mean very little."

"In your opinion."

"This conversation is stupid. Can I hang up now without your twisted brain coming up with some silly, Freudian reason why I won't talk to you?"

He laughed again. "How about I come see you?"

"What? Now?" she asked, panicking.

"Sure, why not? Neither of us can sleep."

"I was sleeping just fine until the stupid phone woke me up."

"Afraid to see me?"

"No." Oh, hell, yes. She did not want to be put in a position of proving to him that he meant nothing to her. And that was exactly what he had in mind. When it came to using her own arguments against her, Sam was a master.

"Then I'll come pick you up. We'll go for a drive."

Great. A drive in the moonlight on a flawless autumn night. "What for?"

"To make absolutely certain there's nothing left between us? What we had was good, Callie, and if there's any chance—"

"There's not. Nothing's changed. In a few weeks you'll be going home to your ranch, and I'll still be here working at the paper."

"So what's the harm of us seeing each other? Maybe we can lay to rest some old ghosts. I'd like to be as certain as you that you were right to turn me down all those years ago."

Was she really that certain? Odd, but the memory of that night he'd proposed hadn't faded one iota in all those years. She'd met him at Sal's on a Friday night, a lush spring evening full of promise. She could still remember how the air smelled, how the breeze felt against her bare arms as she'd climbed out of her beat-up VW Bug, aching to share her good news with Sam. She'd been granted a summer internship at the *Daily Record* over a dozen other students who'd applied. It was an important stepping-stone in her career plans.

But Sam had had news of his own. His uncle had passed on, and Roundrock was now his.

"I'm moving to Nevada, Callie. For good this time. And I want you to come with me."

She stared, a slice of pizza halfway to her mouth, forgotten. *"When?"*

"Now. Well, at the end of the term, I guess."

"I couldn't possibly," she answered automatically. *"I have an internship. My mother is here—she can't get along without me right now."* Callie's father had died less than two years earlier.

Sam shook his head in disbelief. *"Callie, this is our entire future I'm talking about here. I'm asking you to marry me. Be my wife. Share my life, my dreams."*

Marry him? *"And what about my life? Don't my dreams count for anything? I want to be a reporter."*

"And I want to be a rancher. I don't inherit a fifty-thousand-acre spread every day, you know."

She wanted to cry out, I don't get an internship every day, either! But the brag seemed childish, unconvincing. She fell back on an argument any sane person would find convincing. *"We're too young."*

"We've been in love forever," he countered, one of the few times he'd used the L-word. *"Do you think that'll change?"*

"I need time."

He looked so disappointed she wanted to take it back, to throw her arms around him and agree to anything he suggested. She'd fantasized many times of how and when Sam would propose marriage to her. None of her fantasies had resembled this scenario. In her dreams, she'd always been pre-

pared with an enthusiastic "Yes!" But this was reality, and she couldn't make life-altering decisions that quickly. It wasn't her way.

"I don't need time," he said simply. "I want to live the rest of my life with you, Callie. And if you don't feel the same, I need to know now."

"You're saying that if I don't agree to marry you right here and now, I must not love you enough. Is that it?" she asked in utter disbelief. How could he do this to her, give her such unrealistic ultimatums?

"I'm saying you knew this was coming. You knew I'd eventually take over Uncle Ned's ranch. You've had plenty of time to think about it."

That wasn't true. She'd had no idea this day would come so soon. "This is totally unfair. I love you, Sam, but I can't marry you now."

"Why not?"

If he didn't get it by now, she couldn't explain it to him. She shook her head and lowered her gaze, her eyes filling with tears. The next time she looked up, he was gone.

Sam's words over the telephone jerked her back into the present. "I'll pick you up in about twenty minutes."

"Sam, I don't think . . ." He'd hung up. "Great," she muttered. It would serve him right if she stayed in bed and refused to answer the door when he got there. But his solution to that would probably be to pick the lock on her carriage-house apartment and come up after her. The vision gave her goose bumps. No, she didn't need him to find her still in her pj's.

But she was damned if she would primp for him. She pulled on an old pair of jeans, an olive-green T-shirt purchased from the army-navy surplus store, and a pair of thongs. She scraped her hair back into an untidy braid and didn't even contemplate makeup.

She was waiting at the bottom of the enclosed stairs when he pulled up in his rented sedan. She locked her door behind her, pocketed the keys, and climbed into his car. "This reminds me of when we used to sneak out in high school," she said. "Remember how you would pick me up in that old bucket of bolts you called a car?"

Now, why had she brought up that memory? On those occasions when she would climb out her bedroom window to meet Sam in the dark of the night, they always ended up driving to the cemetery and making out.

"Yeah, I remember. I used to love watching you shimmy down that pecan tree by your window. You look so pretty in the moonlight."

Callie's heart stumbled. Was he in the past now, or the present? Surely he couldn't think she looked pretty right now when she'd taken great pains not to.

"Where are we going?" she asked bluntly.

"I don't know. I thought we'd just drive around. Maybe check out that new subdivision that's going in around Hatter's Creek."

"They're building some nice houses over there," she agreed blandly as she fastened her seat belt. In the old days, she would have forgone the belt and scooted next to him. Thank God this car had bucket seats.

They were silent for a while. Callie stole glances at Sam's strong profile, with its bold, straight nose and the shock of caramel hair that habitually flopped over his high forehead. At twenty-eight he was in the prime of his manhood, much more handsome than he'd been at twenty—and more interesting, she admitted. As a youth he'd thought of nothing but horses and cows and rodeos. Now he had a past—a wife who'd left him—and a daughter. Sam Sanger as a doting father was undeniably appealing. Darn hard to resist, in fact.

But for all of the reasons she'd already acknowledged, she had to resist. It would be useless, even harmful, to allow feelings for Sam to bloom. She turned her head and looked out the window at the sleepy town.

"Been dating anyone?" Sam asked.

"Not lately."

"Mom told me you were seeing Randy Muehler a while back."

"Last year. He was still in love with his ex-wife, though, so it didn't work out. How about you?"

"My divorce from Debra was final only a month ago. I haven't had time even to think about dating." Until now. Callie could almost hear the unspoken words reverberating in the car.

"We separated a year ago, but she was gone long before that—in her mind, anyway. I never loved her, not the way I loved you."

"Sam, I don't want to hear this. It's none of my business."

"I'm making it your business, in case you think I'm reeling from a broken heart. I latched onto Debra because she reminded me of you. She was funny and interesting and smart, and so involved in life. But she was fundamentally different in one way."

Curiosity got the best of Callie. "And that was . . . ?"

"She let me talk her into leaving her hometown and

moving to Babcock, Nevada, with me. She was every bit as miserable there as you would have been, I expect."

"I never said I'd be miserable on the ranch, Sam," she argued. "If I had made the decision to live there, I'd have found a way to keep busy and develop interests. But I chose to stay here and follow my own dream. Can you imagine what it would feel like if someone took your ranch away from you? Told you you couldn't ride a horse again?"

He didn't answer, but she could tell from the expression on his face that he didn't like the prospect.

"Without your ranching and your riding, you wouldn't be Sam Sanger anymore. And without my writing and reporting and editing, I wouldn't be Callie Calloway anymore. I'd be . . . someone else. And back then, when I refused to marry you and move to Round-rock, I was desperately afraid of losing that identity."

Amazing, she thought. Eight years ago she'd been so close to the situation, she hadn't been able to under-stand or explain her dread of leaving Destiny and aban-doning her career plans. Now, with a little distance and maturity, she could see things much more clearly.

"You never explained it like that before," Sam said.

"I wasn't able to before."

"And do you still feel the same way? Like if you quit being editor of the *Daily Record* you would lose your-self?"

She sighed. "Not exactly. I used to think being an editor would be all I needed, whether here or in some bigger city. But I've been doing that for a while, and . . ." She couldn't quite put it into words. She was feeling dissatisfied. She'd watched her friends, one by one, get married and start families, and she'd realized that she wanted more than to be an editor in Destiny, Texas. It didn't completely fulfill her.

"Maybe you need a change."

She'd already come to that conclusion. "I've been sending out résumés to the *Dallas Morning News*, the *Houston Chronicle*, even *The Washington Post*. Might as well go for the brass ring."

"Yeah, I reckon you're good enough to work for any paper in the country."

She couldn't detect any strains of sarcasm in his voice, so she thanked him for the compliment. That was the first time she could remember him saying anything nice about her work. "You've been reading the paper, then?"

"I've been reading the paper for years. Mom always sends me the Sunday edition. With your byline highlighted."

"Oh." That tied a knot in Callie's tongue.

Sam gave an evil laugh. "Used to drive Debra nuts."

Callie gasped. "Your mother did that even when you were married? Debra had a right to be angry, having her husband's old girlfriend shoved in her face like that."

"Oh, I don't think it was the fact you were an old girlfriend that bothered her. It was the fact that you were doing what she wished she could do. That you'd been the smart one by turning me down, and she'd been stupid to give everything up and move to the edge of nowhere."

"She was stupid for leaving you," Callie blurted out before she could stop herself. "I mean, leaving your husband and baby . . . I just don't get it."

"Don't you?"

"No!" she said hotly. "If I'd decided to marry you, I'd have honored the commitment. No matter what."

"Then I guess it's a good thing I didn't talk you into marrying me. You'd have been restless, just like Debra, but because you're so loyal you would have stayed."

This time, Callie wasn't sure whether she'd been complimented or insulted. "I probably would have made us both very unhappy—all of us, if we'd had children."

"Maybe. I was much happier after Debra left, knowing that I wasn't keeping her from the things she loved. She moved to Vegas."

"So you're saying we made the right decision after all by not marrying?" Callie asked, almost afraid to hear his answer.

"When I think about it analytically, yeah. You might have adapted to ranch life better than Debra did, but you would've always missed what you gave up. And I would always feel guilty for taking you away from that. But when I put my brain aside and think with my heart . . ."

Callie held her breath.

"Dammit, Callie, I can't imagine being unhappy with you, no matter where we lived or what we were doing."

FOUR

Callie didn't know what to say. Of all things, she hadn't expected such an impassioned declaration. Sam had stopped the car on the side of the road, and he was staring at her with those incredible blue eyes that made her feel like she was standing in a warm summer rain. He licked his lips and unfastened his seat belt. All at once Callie realized he meant to kiss her.

"Sam, no," she said quickly, scrunching as close to the passenger door as she could. "We're not a couple of teenagers anymore."

"I want to kiss you," he said, his voice like black velvet. "I need to kiss you."

"No, Sam. N-O. No more kissing."

Kiss him, said a seductive voice inside her head. It felt as if it came from outside her, yet it was directly between her ears.

"For old time's sake?" he cajoled.

"Right, like I'm going to fall for a clichéd line like

that." But she'd always found it nearly impossible to deny Sam when he was gentle like this.

He reached for her hand. She tried to snatch it away, but she wasn't fast enough, and he captured it, the way a cat might catch a bird, only without the teeth and claws.

"One kiss. I won't ask for more."

Kiss him, the voice said again. *One little kiss won't hurt.*

"Hah! No, Sam. Take me home. Take me home or I'll get out and walk."

He stared at her for several more heartbeats, as if evaluating the situation, trying to find a weakness, a chink in her armor. She pushed her chin forward, hoping against hope he wouldn't find what he was looking for.

"All right," he finally said with a sigh. "I'll take you home. I'm glad we had this talk."

"Me too," she said in a small voice. His capitulation had been too easy. What did he have up his sleeve?

"I understand some things about you that I didn't before—and maybe about me too."

"Good."

"Maybe we can be friends."

"I'd like that." *But I'd really like to go to bed with you.* Ack! Where had that come from? Was she going crazy, hearing voices in her head?

She said nothing more until he pulled up the driveway that led to her apartment. "Don't stay away from my mom just 'cause I'm hanging around. I'll behave myself, I promise."

"No more kisses?" she asked warily.

"Not unless you want them." She could have sworn his eyes twinkled in the darkness.

"All right, then. Friends." She held out her hand. He took it. *Kiss him!* the voice said again, more insistent this time.

She yanked open the car door and fled.

Once she was safely inside, watching as Sam's taillights turned out of the driveway and disappeared into the night, she had to congratulate herself. She'd held out, she'd been in control. She'd resisted temptation. She should be very proud of herself for being so strong.

But as she climbed back into her nightgown she noticed that her nipples were hard and aching, her mouth dry, her hands and arms empty feeling. Just what, exactly, had she accomplished by acting like a priggish maid, except to deny herself the unequaled bliss of kissing Sam Sanger?

The next time Callie's phone rang, she was again asleep. Her eyes still closed, she grabbed for the phone on the nightstand, missing with her first couple of reaches. Finally she managed to get the receiver to her ear. "Hullo?"

"Callie, it's Sloan Bennett. Did I call too early?"

She cracked one eye open and squinted at her clock radio. Almost seven-thirty. She should have been up an hour ago! She struggled for alertness. "No, no, it's not too early." She sat up in bed and rubbed her face. "Is something wrong?"

"It's about what you said last night—you know, about Johnny Sanger. It's been bugging me. So early this morning I had a talk with Danny Fowler. He says that some things about the suicide scenario bothered him too."

"Yeah? Like, what kind of things?" Callie dragged the phone into the bathroom and started brushing her teeth. Sloan would have to understand.

"Like the fact that he killed himself with a shotgun, when there was a perfectly good pistol in his file drawer. Given the choice, a pistol would be more logical—easier to manage."

"Uh-huh," she said, her mouth full of toothpaste.

"Also, a man using a shotgun to kill himself puts the barrel in his mouth ninety percent of the time. Johnny shot himself in the chest. And the gun was fired at close range, but it wasn't a contact wound."

Callie rinsed her mouth. "In other words, he didn't press the barrel against himself."

"Right. Nothing shocking about all this, but it makes the hair on the back of my neck stand up. You know?"

"Yeah." That described her feelings exactly. "I appreciate your call, Sloan."

"Well, I didn't call just to pass on information. In fact, I had a specific reason for catching you at home. We—that is, Danny and me—were thinking we didn't want anyone else to know about this, at least, not right away."

"Oh, don't worry," Callie said. "I wouldn't print anything this insubstantial. Are you saying the Sanger file is still open?"

"Unofficially. The chief isn't wild about us devoting

a lot of time or manpower to it, though. Which brings me to our request."

"Uh-oh." Callie was sure she wasn't going to like this.

"Could you do some snooping for us?"

"Oh, gee, Sloan, I don't know. . . ."

"Danny says you've done this kind of thing for the department before. And we're not asking you to go out of your way. Just, if the opportunity presents itself, ask a few questions. Keep your eyes open. You're friends with the Sangers. They won't think twice about the fact that you're hanging around."

"But I really didn't intend to 'hang around.' "

Sloan was silent for a moment. "Okay, I get it. You don't want to see that much of Sam."

Callie didn't like disappointing Sloan this way, especially when he'd been so forthcoming the night before. "Look, I can't make any promises. But I'll do what I can." Shoot, she'd already told Beverly she'd snoop around. Might as well put Sloan in the loop. "If I hear or notice anything, I'll give you a call."

"That's all we're asking." Sloan sounded relieved.

"Do you have any, um, suspects in mind? Anyone you think might benefit from Johnny's death?"

"Ohhhh, yeah. With that million-dollar life-insurance policy, anyone in that family. Beverly Sanger is about to be a very rich woman, and I can't imagine that she won't share with her kin."

"At least Beverly will be taken care of," Callie murmured. "Oh, speaking of suicide, the policy was sitting right out on Johnny's desk, right?"

"Uh-huh. Mighty convenient evidence of a suicide motive."

Again Sloan had made Callie's point for her. He was a sharp one.

"Look," he said, "I won't keep you. I'm supposed to be out on patrol. Just wanted to drop that bug in your ear."

"If something falls in my lap, I'll clue you in," she said, just to be sure they were clear. "But I won't go digging around unless I have something more to go on—mostly because the Sangers are friends, and I can't take advantage of that."

"Understood. Thanks, Callie."

Callie hung up and looked at the clock again. Hell, she was going to be late to the city council meeting, something that really irritated her boss, who no doubt would also be there because he liked to see and be seen. She'd overslept, big time. She could thank Sam for that.

She opened the door to the little balcony off her bedroom. It was hard to know how to dress this time of year, but the breeze that caressed her naked body felt pretty warm for a late-October morning. She showered, threw on some cotton slacks and a long-sleeved striped blouse, then, still barefoot, grabbed a pair of socks and her makeup case and ran down the stairs to the garage. She was pretty sure she had some loafers in the trunk of her car.

During the ten-minute drive to the municipal building, where the council met, she finally had time to ruminate on Sloan's phone call. If someone in Sam's family was guilty of murder, it would have to be Will, wouldn't it? Beverly and Tamra had gone to the store together and had found Johnny's body when they returned. Will, on the other hand, had been close by, working in the fields. He could have done the deed while Beverly and Tamra were gone.

Callie didn't consider Sam, because even if she hadn't known he was incapable of violence, he'd been in Nevada at the time. He would have had to hire someone. . . . Okay, her cool reporter's brain said that was possible. Maybe the farm was more of a financial drain on his own operation than she'd imagined.

"Oh, come off it," she murmured.

Will's little wife was a more likely suspect than Sam, and Callie couldn't imagine Tamra having the strength to lift a shotgun, much less wrestle it into Johnny's hands and force him to shoot himself—which is what would have had to happen.

The idea of Beverly killing her husband for the insurance was ludicrous. Callie didn't waste her time considering it. In fact, she decided, all this talk of murder was ridiculous. She pushed thoughts of the matter aside. The council was going to discuss a new proposed zoning ordinance, and she was woefully unprepared.

After parking illegally in the overflowing parking lot, praying she wouldn't get a ticket, Callie discovered she didn't have any shoes, not even sneakers, in her car. Damn, damn, damn. She'd never covered a story with bare feet, but there was a first time for everything.

The proceedings had already started by the time she made it inside the building. She grabbed the first empty chair she saw and sat down. She slapped a fresh tape into her recorder and pushed the record button.

Within moments someone sat down next to her.

Callie scooted over a bit to give the newcomer room. Then her breath caught in her throat. At first she thought she was imagining things. But she couldn't be mistaken. That distinctive, masculine scent could come from only one person. But even without the scent, she'd have known it was Sam. His body seemed to have an electrical field around it that did something to her personal ions.

"What are you doing here?" she asked without looking up. She imagined those blue eyes gazing at her, and her insides quivered.

"I'm an interested citizen."

"You came here to harass me."

A man in front of them turned and glared.

Sam lowered his voice to a whisper, putting his mouth right next to Callie's ear. "You owe me a kiss."

"I'm busy," she groused, trying to pay attention to the discussion about improvements to the municipal building. It was bad enough he'd stolen her sleep with his impromptu visit, then invaded her dreams. Did he have to interfere with her work as well?

"Actually, I came to show my support for Alan Buntz. He's arguing against that zoning ordinance that would allow commercial business in our neighborhood."

"Oh." She was ashamed at the disappointment she felt. Had she really thought Sam had come here specifically seeking her out?

The man in front of them turned around to glare again, so they kept quiet during the remainder of the dull meeting. Sam raised his hand when the discussion about the zoning came up, and he expressed himself eloquently, pleading that the council protect the peaceful, bucolic atmosphere of his neighborhood, which was about all it had going for it. That and a farming history that went back to before Texas was a state.

The council voted the zoning measure down.

"You gonna quote me in the paper?" Sam asked when he noticed Callie taking notes.

"It's news when someone who doesn't even live permanently in Destiny can single-handedly sway the city council. Oh, don't get your shorts in a knot. It'll be a one-column story on page three of the Metropolitan section. You have a real phobia about the press, don't you? Even if it's good press."

He shrugged. "I'm entitled."

"I suppose you are."

He looked down and frowned. "What happened to your shoes?"

"Don't ask."

"I heard you had dinner with Sloan Bennett last night."

She had to stifle a giggle. She hadn't seriously imagined that she and Sloan would become the subject of gossip. "Yes, I did," she replied, deliberately mysterious.

"I thought you weren't dating anyone."

"Sloan and I aren't dating." She paused, then added, "That was business."

"Something to do with my father's death? I read in your story that Bennett was the first cop to arrive on the scene."

Callie considered lying. She wasn't obligated to talk about her behind-the-scenes research. But considering Sam's understandable paranoia about the newspaper, she decided to tell him some version of the truth. "We did discuss your father. I was tying up some loose ends. I have no plans to write anything more about it," she added. "But, Sam, I have to be honest with you. The police aren't positive your father killed himself, and I have my suspicions too."

Sam stared at her in utter consternation. "Excuse me?"

"There are some things that don't add up."

Thunderclouds moved across his face. "Are you insinuating someone killed him?" he said in a ferocious whisper.

"It's a possibility. Look, I shouldn't have even told you. But I didn't want it to come out of left field if it turns into a real murder investigation."

"You mean if suddenly there's a story splashed across the front page announcing my dad's murder? Thanks for the warning." He started to turn away.

"Sam, wait. You don't understand. This has nothing to do with my job at the paper."

"Then what exactly *is* your role, huh, Callie? Just an average, concerned citizen?" Fury rolled off him in waves. She could feel them washing over her.

She hadn't meant to make him angry. She'd just wanted to be honest with him, because she didn't like deceiving him. "Will you let me explain what's going on?"

He took a deep breath, seeming to get hold of his temper. "Okay."

As she gathered her thoughts, wanting to choose just the right words, she noticed her boss staring her down from across the room. "Um, this isn't really the time or the place to discuss a sensitive matter, and I have to get back to work. Can I call you?"

Stubbornly he shook his head. "I want you to look me in the eye when you explain why you're mucking around in something that ought to be left alone. Don't you know the pain such groundless speculation could cause my mother?"

Callie didn't dare tell Sam it was his own mother who was most suspicious. "Tonight."

"What?"

"Come over tonight and I'll explain things to you. Don't look at me like that. I'm not asking you out on a date." Or had she? He didn't appear so angry anymore. In fact, the look he gave her was hot enough to melt her fillings.

She glanced around nervously. At least no one other than her boss was staring at them, or blatantly eavesdropping. "I've really got to go," she tried again. "Tonight? I'll meet you on neutral ground if you want."

"I'll come to your house," he finally agreed.

"Okay, then." That gave her the rest of the day to figure out what she would tell him.

Callie tried, she really did, to concentrate on the damn city council story. But she hadn't done this type of mundane reporting in a long time, and the words that should have come automatically from her brain to her fingertips to the computer screen now had to be dragged one laborious syllable at a time.

"You were late to the council meeting this morning, Miss Calloway."

Callie jumped, not having expected company. She'd left instructions with her secretary that she wasn't to be disturbed until this dumb story was finished. Unfortunately, nothing was going to keep Tom Winers, publisher of the *Destiny Daily Record*, out of her office if that's where he wanted to be.

"Morning, Tom," she said after taking a fortifying gulp of cold coffee. She didn't have time for this.

She and her boss had never enjoyed the best of employer/employee relationships. After the *Record*'s former editor had moved on, Tom had stepped into the man's rather large shoes and had all but driven the paper out of business with his brand of "journalism," learned from tabloid talk shows, no doubt. The staff was desperate for anyone to take over the reins, and Callie was the most qualified.

She and Tom both knew he'd promoted her more because of pressure from the rest of the staff than because he harbored any real faith in her abilities.

Even now, two years after she'd moved her things into the editor's office, Tom was still trying to trip her up so he could prove he had been right all along and reinstall himself as editor.

"Is there something I can do for you, Tom?" She glanced at her watch, thinking about deadlines and her jam-packed schedule for the rest of the day.

"You certainly can. You can tell me why you're locked up here in your ivory tower doing a routine story any intern could handle. You have more important responsibilities. Like wearing shoes."

Callie didn't respond to the rib. "Joey's sick with the flu, Emma's on vacation, and Eloise is covering the cattle auction over at the fairgrounds. Unless I wanted to send Amelia to the city council meeting—" Amelia was their volunteer "social editor."

"All right, I get the picture. Still, I don't think you should make yourself inaccessible to the public. Your job involves a certain amount of public relations."

"Fine. If anyone needs to see me—"

"Someone does. Herman Johnson's daughter."

"Nicole? What does she want?"

"Damned if I know. But your secretary told her you were too busy to see her. And if you're so damned busy you can't see the police chief's daughter, then you might think about resisting the temptation to schmooze with your old boyfriend on company time!" On that note he stormed out of her office.

"Whew-boy," Callie muttered. Then she buzzed her secretary. "Denise, is Nicole Johnson still here?"

"Uh-huh."

"Could you send her in, please?"

"Sure thing."

Moments later Chief Johnson's oft-married, oft-divorced daughter sidled into the room. She was in her late thirties, but she dressed as if she were ten or fifteen years younger. "I know this must be a bad time, and I wouldn't bother you if it weren't important," she said to Callie, tugging on the hem of her bright green minidress. Her hair was uncharacteristically mussed and her normally bright pink lipstick mostly chewed off.

"It's okay, Nicole." Callie sensed the woman needed a friend. She didn't seem to have any—at least, not any female ones. "I need a break, anyway." She stayed behind her desk, hoping Nicole didn't notice her bare feet.

She was planning on stopping by home during her lunch break to find some shoes.

"This won't take long. You did such a nice job on that story about Johnny Sanger's s-suicide." Her voice broke on the last word. She cleared her throat. "I was just wondering, since you know the Sangers and you've spent some time with them lately, if you weren't privy to some information that didn't make it into print."

Callie's instincts went on red alert. "What kind of information?" she asked casually.

"Well, you know, about his will, and his insurance. Stuff like that."

"Nicole, even if I did know something about the Sangers' private affairs, I wouldn't go telling everybody about it."

"Oh, not everybody, of course," Nicole said. "But I have a sort of . . . special interest. You see, Johnny promised . . . well, he indicated that he wouldn't forget me. I believed him. Johnny was a man of his word, and if he said he'd take care of me . . . I'm just afraid that when his wife finds out, she'll lie or somehow do me out of what Johnny wanted for me."

Callie knew her eyes had grown bigger and bigger with every word Nicole had uttered. Good God, surely she wasn't saying . . .

"I can tell what you're thinking, and it's not that way at all. Johnny and me were friends, that's all. He needed someone to talk to, someone who wouldn't judge him or expect anything from him except a little conversation, companionship. You know?"

Yes, Callie was afraid she did know. "You were

friends with him a long time, I imagine." She tried her best to screen the mounting horror out of her voice.

"A few months, that's all. But I got to know him well. He was a fine man. I can't believe . . ." Nicole's eyes overflowed. "Why didn't he tell me he was considering such a damn-fool thing? I'd have talked him out of it."

Callie handed Nicole a tissue. "Nicole, I'm really sorry, but I can't talk about Johnny's private affairs. But as for the will and the insurance, they'll be filed with the court, you know, and if he did leave you something, you'll be notified. No one can keep it from you."

"Really?"

"Really. And I promise, if I hear anything that directly affects you, I'll let you know, okay?"

"That'd be nice. Thanks, Callie."

Callie shuffled her out of the office as quickly as she could, then collapsed behind her desk. Oh, God, this couldn't be. Johnny Sanger was having an affair with Nicole Johnson? No wonder Chief Johnson wanted his men to close this case and forget about it.

Reluctantly, she picked up the phone and dialed the police. They patched her through to Sloan's cellular phone, which he carried with him while on patrol, and she asked him to call her back on a pay phone. She didn't trust the cellular to be a secure line.

"Callie, what's up?" he asked her less than a minute later.

"Sloan?" she said, feeling a little sick. "I have another piece of information for you. But you have to swear on a stack of Bibles you'll keep this to yourself if it doesn't have a bearing on the case."

◆━━━◆

"Sam, why don't you let me take care of Deana for you while you're out tonight," Tamra offered.

"You don't have to do that," Sam said. "I don't mind hiring a sitter. Millicent Jones's younger sister—"

"Oh, why pay someone when you have me? I'd love the chance to spend a little extra time with my sweet niece. Will and I want to have children—lots of children."

"That's real nice of you, Tamra." This was the first time his brother's soft-spoken little wife had said more than two words to him. "If you're sure it's no bother."

"None at all. Will and I will take her to McDonald's. Kids seem to love that place."

Oh, yeah. They didn't have McDonald's in Babcock, Nevada. But like a heat-seeking missile, Deana had discovered Ronald and Happy Meals within twenty-four hours of her arrival in Destiny.

"C'mon, Deana," Tamra said in her exaggerated Southern accent. "Don't you want to spend the evening with your aunt Tamra?"

With uncharacteristic shyness, Deana shook her head and hid her face against her father's pants leg.

Sam reassured the child and handed her over to his sister-in-law. Deana didn't cry, but she stuck out her lower lip in a thoroughly manipulative way.

Sam did his best to ignore her. "I'll pick her up, say, around eleven?"

"Make it midnight. I know you and Callie have a lot of catching up to do." Her expression was sly. Sometimes Sam wondered if his whole family was in cahoots, trying to play matchmaker.

As he drove to Callie's, he tried to picture what kind of mood he would find her in this time. Would that determined chin of hers be thrust out, challenging him to argue with her? And what type of explanation could she possibly give that would excuse her trying to dig up dirt on his father?

Wistfully, he thought about the old Callie he'd caught a glimpse of on their late-night outing a few days ago—smiling, teasing, reminiscing. He doubted he'd see that side of her anymore.

So why was he even bothering?

Curiosity, maybe. Lust, definitely, though it was pure idiocy to imagine anything would come of that, not when Callie wouldn't even let him kiss her.

Maybe it was just that the two of them were an unfinished book, a big question mark. He wanted to tie up the loose ends so he could get on with his life. He wanted closure.

He wanted to be able to let her go.

Maybe he was crazy, thinking that seeing more of her would allow him the release he sought. But he was willing to try.

It took several minutes for Callie to answer her door, long enough that Sam peeked into the carriage house to see if her car was there. It was, and he'd actually started to worry about things like slipping in the bathtub when she finally made an appearance.

"Callie?" He got the distinct impression that something was out of kilter.

"Hi, Sam, come on up." Her voice was subdued, her face devoid of expression. "I'm running a little late."

"A little?" he couldn't help saying. She was still in her bathrobe, her hair wrapped in a towel.

"I fell asleep in the bathtub, okay?" she snapped as she led the way up the stairs, her hips swaying beneath pink terry cloth. Damn, she was the only woman he knew who could look alluring in such a getup. She left a delightful scent in her wake, too, like . . .

"Strawberry?"

"What?"

"Did you use strawberry bubble bath?"

"I, um, don't remember. I think so." She opened the door at the top of the enclosed stairway and let him into the living room.

Even if he hadn't known where he was, he'd have picked this place as belonging to Callie Calloway. Cluttered without being messy, she'd filled her cozy living quarters with little things that spoke volumes about her personality—a Rolling Stones poster on one wall and a Mozart poster on another; a set of flowered plates displayed in an old-fashioned bamboo hutch, which sat right next to an ultramodern stereo system.

"Great apartment," he said. "It suits you." Better than his cavernous ranch house with its stiff, Early American antiques suited him, he supposed. He found himself wondering what she would think of the life he'd made for himself—whether she would find it fitting, or be surprised.

"Thanks. Just sit down anywhere. There are some magazines. . . ." Her voice trailed off. "I'll try to hurry."

His attention turned abruptly to Callie again. "Is something wrong?"

She sighed. "Is it that obvious?"

"Callie, honey, what is it?" The endearment slipped out. He didn't care. He did stop himself from going closer, touching her.

"I lost my job." The stark sentence hung in the room like macabre black party streamers.

FIVE

Sam wasn't sure he'd heard right. "You mean the paper's closing?" Maybe that was it. What with paper costs up, advertising revenue down—

"No, Sam, I got fired. Canned."

"What for?"

Callie flopped into an old wingback chair. Within three seconds a yellow-striped cat jumped into her lap. She stroked it absently. "Winers found out I've been applying for jobs elsewhere. Apparently some jackass at one of the papers where I sent my résumé decided to check references without asking me first."

"You're looking for another job?" Sam remembered that sense of dissatisfaction she'd communicated about the *Record* earlier in the day, but he could hardly imagine her working anywhere else.

"I can't—couldn't—stay there forever, not if I want to advance. I've been sending résumés to various big newspapers once a year ever since I graduated from college. It's a ritual. Tom acts like it's some kind of heresy, or that I'm a traitor, for even thinking of looking for another job."

"So one of these bigger papers nibbled on your résumé?"

"Apparently. It's happened before, but I've never gotten an offer."

"Do you know which paper is interested?"

"Hah! Like Tom would tell me. Anyway, I'm sure now that they've talked to Tom, they think I'm poison."

She had a point. "Still, you could find out if you did a little detective work—"

"Oh, Sam, I can't deal with that right now. Maybe next week."

Of course. What was he thinking? She'd been at the *Daily Record* for, what, ten years now? She'd served two or three summers as an intern, working for slave wages, fetching coffee and opening mail. After graduation she'd been hired as a full-fledged employee—editing the daily events calendar. She'd quickly earned a real reporter's job.

Tom Winers had just thrown that history down the drain, the jerk. Maybe this would turn into a blessing in disguise for Callie. She'd hinted earlier that it was time for a change. But he couldn't expect her to focus on anything right now except the loss.

"I'm sorry, Callie. I don't know what to say, except that you're fully entitled to be angry and upset, and if you want to cry or hit something or throw things, you can. I won't tease you."

She gave a halfhearted laugh. "Are you kidding? I've been doing most of that all afternoon. In fact, I've been a real bad sport about this. Tom gave me a week's notice, but I boxed up my things and was out of there within twenty minutes, leaving him to explain."

"Bravo. Exactly the way it should have been handled."

"And I've been moaning and groaning and whining ever since."

"And you forgot I was coming over," he added. He acted put out, which was only a slight exaggeration. He'd been thinking of nothing else but this evening all day.

She shook her head vehemently. "I did not. Why do you think I got into the bathtub in the first place? I wanted to calm down before you got here, pretend nothing was wrong, and I thought a nice hot bath would help. Unfortunately it helped too well. I really did fall asleep. *Some*body interrupted my sleep last night." She softened the gibe with a winsome smile.

"I believe you."

"I'm sorry I'm in such a state."

"It's okay, Callie. Like I said, you're entitled."

"Would you mind if we postponed our talk? I'm not thinking very straight right now, and—"

"Yes, fine, we'll postpone it." He wasn't sure why he was behaving so charitably toward her all of a sudden. He supposed it was because she was hurting, and he couldn't stand to see that, much less add to it.

"I could meet you tomorrow for lunch," she suggested.

"Mmm, might not be able to get a sitter. We'll see." He watched her, waiting to see what she would say or do next. She looked so vulnerable with that heated blush on her cheeks, all wrapped up in fuzzy pink terry, that he felt a tremendous urge to hold her, protect her from the world.

But he stopped himself in time. He could think of no woman who needed less protecting. Instead of touching her, he placed his hands on the chair arms and leaned forward until he was nose to nose with her. "How about a pizza from Sal's?"

He could almost see her mouth water. "Sal's?"

"And when I go to pick it up I'll stop by the video store and rent some movies."

"*Casablanca*?" she suggested hopefully.

"That tearjerker? No way. You need something to cheer you up, not make you cry." Besides, he wasn't sure they were ready to watch a romance, much less a tragic one. "How about some Marx Brothers?"

She nodded. "Okay. And maybe an action movie?"

"Perfect."

"The number for Sal's is by the phone, along with the emergency numbers for police and fire."

"Of course. Where else would it be?"

She smiled again, a little more convincingly this time. "Deep-dish sausage and mushroom, and to hell with fat grams."

Funny how the whole tenor of the evening had changed in a few short minutes, Sam mused as he waited for Sal's to answer the phone. He was sorry Callie had lost her job, but a small part of him was glad because it would give them the chance to talk about anything and everything and nothing important. Maybe they could get through the evening without arguing. As for postponing the explanation he'd demanded from her, he wasn't sure he really wanted to know her thoughts on his father's death. Just being with Callie was more soothing than talking the subject to shreds.

He and Callie had always been there for each other during times of adversity. Somehow, when one of them was hurting, all quarrels were forgotten. He remembered the time her father had passed away from an unexpected heart attack. Sam and Callie had fought the week before and were officially "broken-up." But the moment he'd heard about Mr. Calloway, Sam had gone to Callie. She'd accepted his presence and his comfort without question, and whatever stupid thing they'd fought about—he couldn't remember it now—had melted into insignificance.

"Sal's, please hold," a voice said.

It was his own father's death that had brought her back to him this time. Only he hadn't accepted her attempts to comfort as readily as he should have. Looking back a few days, he was truly ashamed of the hostile way he'd treated her. Oh, he wasn't ready to take her completely at face value. She was still a journalist first, job or no job. But she'd been very perceptive when she'd accused him of holding on to the bitterness from their last breakup.

"Sal's, can I take your order?" The voice belonged to Sal himself.

"Yeah, hi, Sal. I need a large sausage-and-mushroom deep dish to go—"

"Sam? Sam Sanger?"

"Uh, yeah."

"Wow, I thought I'd gone back in time there for a minute. Don't tell me. It's for you and Callie, right?"

"Right." He hoped Callie didn't mind if people gossiped about them.

Sal laughed. "You two are as predictable as sunshine on the Fourth of July. Same order, every Friday night. I got to where I didn't even wait for you to call in the order, remember?"

"Yeah, I remember." He was remembering a lot of things. He and Callie'd had some good times. The ache of nostalgia squeezed his chest. But it was only nostalgia, he cautioned himself. They couldn't throw their quarrels out the window like they used to. Their differences were too fundamental these days.

"Okay, I've got you down," Sal said. "Pizza'll be ready in about twenty minutes."

"Great, I'll be there to get it."

Before returning to the living room, Sam rummaged around in the red-and-white-tiled kitchen for some things he knew Callie would have—a pretty china cup, some herbal tea, a kettle. He filled the kettle and set it on the stove, then put a tea bag in the cup.

"The water should boil in a few minutes," he told Callie as he put on his denim jacket. She hadn't moved since he'd left the room to order the pizza. "I put out some tea for you. Raspberry and chamomile. I'll be back in half an hour."

He started to walk out the door, but at the last moment he strode quickly to her chair, leaned down, and kissed her too pale cheek. He wanted to do more, but decided not to push his luck. "Chin up, Callie. You're strong, and you can get through this."

❧———————❧

As soon as Sam was gone, Callie released a pent-up sigh. A few minutes ago she'd been in a state of panic, wishing there was some way she could call off this . . . meeting, or whatever it was if it wasn't a date. She'd even started to phone him as her mind scurried around looking for some believable excuse. But she'd hung up before the connection was even made. She'd known Sam wouldn't be put off by anything. He was too damned determined.

She didn't need the extra stress of dealing with Sam right now, she'd told herself when the bell had rung. Didn't she have enough on her plate? But the moment she saw him, everything had changed. He'd always been there during her worst times, even when she didn't deserve his devotion. During disasters, he made sure she ate, he rubbed her shoulders, he bolstered her spirits. Suddenly she felt silly for having dreaded Sam's arrival. He was so easy to talk to—when he wanted to be—and unburdening herself had come as naturally as breathing.

He had uncanny abilities, Sam did. He could make her feel awful with one cold look, as he had at the cemetery. And he could also make the hurt feel better with a touch, a smile. She rubbed her hand against her cheek where he'd kissed her, and a pleasurable shiver wiggled down her spine.

Already she felt better, just knowing that someone understood her position and took her side. She pushed Grits—the cat—from her lap, opened the antique wardrobe that held her TV and VCR and positioned them just right, dusted off the remote control, and threw some pillows on the floor by the coffee table. There, she'd arranged things just like when they were kids, watching the midnight fright movie at her parents' house.

He would be back soon. She went to her bedroom and, after contemplating a slinky lounging outfit, chose a comfy, nonsexy hot-pink sweatsuit. She combed out her wet hair and powdered her nose, which was still a little red from crying.

The incredible aroma of Sal's pizza preceded Sam up the stairs. Callie's stomach rumbled and her chest tightened. She was either very excited about the pizza, or more excited about her evening with Sam than she had any right to be.

"You moved," he said with a note of surprise when he entered the room. "And you put on clothes. You didn't have to."

Callie was pouring Coke over two glasses of ice. "It happens from time to time." She spied the Blockbuster Video sack. "What movies did you rent?"

"*Duck Soup* and, um, Stallone. Can't remember which one. They all seem the same to me."

"Blessedly, predictably the same. That's why they're so popular. The good guys always win."

"You don't think they're popular because a lot of stuff gets blown up?" Sam set the pizza box on the coffee table.

"Good point."

They dimmed the lights, put on *Duck Soup*, and gorged on pizza and mindless slapstick for the next hour and a half. Sam held her hand, and she let him. He played with her hair, braiding it, combing it with his fingers. She let him do that, too, because it seemed to have a calming effect on her. She even let him put his arm around her and pull her against him, so that she rested her head on his shoulder.

By the time the credits were running for the Stallone movie, it was getting late, and Callie expected him to try to kiss her. She had her defenses all lined up, too, all the reasons they shouldn't take this trip down memory lane any further.

He surprised the heck out of her when he withdrew his arm, sat up, and stretched. "I should go and let you get some sleep."

"Hmm, I'm not sure I'll sleep much tonight anyway." She took off her glasses and rubbed her eyes. "Too much to think about."

"Then you want me to stay?" He smiled innocently.

"No! Um, that is—"

"Don't waste a good argument. I have to leave, anyway. I said I would pick up Deana before midnight."

"Pick her up? I thought your mother would take care of her."

Sam shook his head. "Deana's with my brother and sister-in-law. Tamra volunteered, and I think my mom wanted some time to herself."

Callie felt a moment of unease. Will Sanger was her prime murder suspect. She shook off the discomfort. Surely Deana was perfectly safe, especially with Tamra there.

"Is there anything else I can do for your mom?" Callie asked. "I'd be happy to run errands or make phone calls."

"The nicest thing you can do for her is refrain from writing anything else about Dad's death for the paper," Sam answered gruffly.

Callie sighed. "Sam, even if I wanted to write about you or your family, I don't work for the newspaper anymore, remember? You can relax."

Sam put a hand to his forehead. "Sorry," he murmured. "I can't seem to get over being paranoid about that paper."

"Worrying about the paper, I can understand. But me?"

"You're an ambitious reporter, Callie."

"Yeah, but I go after the bad guys. I don't prey on my friends."

"Your friends could get hurt in the fallout."

There was no denying the truth in his observation. Still, she hated ending such an enjoyable evening on a sour note. She touched his shoulder, then his face. "I appreciate the pizza and the movies—emotional first aid."

He smiled, then clasped her hand and brought the palm to his lips, holding it there for a moment while Callie held her breath. She'd never imagined that part of her body could be so sensitive.

"Callie, do you want me to kiss you?"

"Umm . . ." She couldn't think. Her brain had just gone numb.

" 'Cause I will, if that's what you want. I was trying not to take advantage of the situation—you being all upset about your job and everything."

Her job. She'd managed to forget the horror of being fired for a few hours, but now the misery came pouring back into her mind. Tears pressed at the back of her eyes, and she wanted more than anything for Sam to hold her, kiss her, consume her with the heat of passion.

Apparently it wasn't necessary for her to answer his question in words. Something in her face must have given her assent, because before she knew what was happening, her body was plastered against his and his mouth was on hers, the kiss searing her clear to her soul. He wrapped her hair around his hands and gently pulled, forcing her head back to give him fuller access to her mouth. His arousal pushed insistently against her abdomen in a way that made his intentions—or at least his desires—abundantly clear.

She broke the kiss only long enough to blurt out, "Stay with me, Sam." Then she was kissing him again, savoring the feel of his hair as she sifted it with her fingers, reveling in the heat and hardness of his body, drinking up his intensity.

Eventually the kiss gentled. He nuzzled her neck, her ear, and then whispered, "Did you just ask me to stay with you?"

"Mm, those words did seem to come out of my mouth."

"I would if I could."

"Oh." Of course he couldn't stay. He had other responsibilities, like a two-year-old daughter. "Just as well. I . . . I don't know what I was thinking. I guess I just don't look forward to being alone with my thoughts."

"You could come home with me. Stay in the guest room. Mom would understand."

"That's all your mother needs is a houseguest. No, Sam, I think we'd better say good night now. I shouldn't have gotten so carried away."

"That's your opinion. I like it when you get carried

away." He looked down at her, his confused emotions spilling into his face. He appeared strong and determined and achingly vulnerable all at the same time, and for a split second she almost decided to leave with him, to cling to him and never let him out of her sight again.

After a moment, though, sanity reasserted itself. "I'm a big girl. I'll stay by myself."

"I'll call you tomorrow." His hand slid down her back to squeeze her bottom much too familiarly before he turned and disappeared down the dark tunnel of the stairway. She turned on a light, followed him down, then firmly locked the door behind him.

She had this feeling that she'd just made a narrow escape, but only a temporary one.

Callie spent Saturday writing letters of application to various newspapers. She couldn't afford to stay unemployed for long. She even decided to apply to the *Las Vegas Review-Journal & Sun*. If she was going to move anyway, would it be such a bad thing to move closer to Sam?

She'd never admitted this to anyone, but the thought of leaving Destiny and living in a big city terrified her. Here in her hometown she was someone important. Everyone knew her, and most, she believed, respected her. If she moved to Houston or Dallas or D.C., she'd be a very little fish in a huge pond. Even while she was sending out all those résumés over the years, she knew she could always turn down a job if one presented itself.

Now she didn't have that luxury. She either had to

move up and away, or stay here and get a job doing something besides reporting. The latter simply wasn't an option.

She also spent a good portion of the day staring at the phone, willing it to ring. Sam had said he would call, and he'd never broken his word to her.

When he finally did call, her relief and elation quickly dulled. He'd only wanted to check and see if she was doing all right. He didn't linger on the phone, and he didn't ask to see her again or press her about Johnny's death, which left Callie feeling more than vaguely disappointed. Kissing Sam was like eating M&M's; she couldn't stop at just one, and the more she indulged, the more she wanted.

Sunday she went quietly stir-crazy. She wasn't used to being idle.

By Monday she was full of purpose again. She went to the copy shop, spent a fortune on stamps, and sent out her résumés and clippings. Then she went to her favorite frozen-yogurt shop and indulged in a fat-free hot fudge sundae.

She knew almost everyone who came into the store, and most stopped at her table to chat a minute. If she were sitting in an ice-cream shop in some big city, she probably wouldn't know a single person who walked in.

Well, she'd have to get used to things like that. And things like always locking her door, and installing a car alarm in her Nissan, and rush-hour traffic jams and smog and not being able to see the stars at night . . .

"Oh, stop it," she murmured to herself. She was depressing herself. Instead, she thought about Sam, which was only slightly less depressing since he hadn't called again. It was really better that way, she kept telling herself.

But, dammit, she wanted to see him; there was no denying it. All she knew was that she was hurting, and he was the only thing that made her feel better. Sam was her Band-Aid, her temporary fix to a complicated problem.

The situation was hopeless. Nothing had changed. Sam would eventually return to Nevada, and who knew where she would end up. Nonetheless, if she could have conjured him up with sheer will alone, she'd have done it in a second. She would take her comfort where she could get it, and worry about future hurts later.

Two days later Callie couldn't stand it anymore. She showed up at the Sangers' house, unannounced. Just dropping by to see how everyone was getting along, she told Beverly, letting them know she was thinking about them.

"We're doing as well as can be expected." Beverly ushered Callie inside, taking her jacket. "I understand you've got problems of your own, though."

Callie waved away Beverly's concern. "It's just a job. A job's nothing. I can always get another one."

"Sam's putting Deana down for her nap. He'll be down shortly, I'm sure."

"Really, I came to see you."

Beverly's face took on an expression of alarm. "You found something out about—"

"No, no," Callie said hastily. "I mean, I did talk to Officer Bennett, and he agrees that we shouldn't jump to any conclusions one way or another about Johnny's death."

"He doesn't think I'm nuts for asking questions?"

"No. But he doesn't know anything definite, either."

"Didn't they find anything in his office?" she asked a bit desperately. "They spent over an hour in there. . . ."

Callie didn't tell Beverly that an hour was a relatively short time for an evidence team to spend at a crime scene. "Bennett didn't mention anything."

"They made a big mess, you know, with that black powder all over everything, leaving their trash on the floor. I haven't had the energy to clean it up yet. I just shut the door and tried to forget what I saw in there." Her face looked tight with pain. "Tamra offered to do it, but I told her no, not yet."

"Oh, Beverly, no one in the family should have to take care of that. We'll call a cleaning service, okay?"

"Maybe that would be best. If it's not too expensive—oh, dear, I guess I don't really have to worry about that, not with a million-dollar check on the way. I wish I could just send it back. Doesn't feel right, benefiting from Johnny's death that way. Especially since . . ."

"Since what?" Callie prompted.

Beverly sighed. "I told you a fib before. Johnny and I were having some problems. Personal problems. But it was nothing huge," she added quickly, "just little misunderstandings. Sometimes when he was upset with me, I couldn't get him to talk. But I would never . . . I should have appreciated him more when he was alive, that's all. He was a good husband."

Callie's thoughts strayed to Nicole Johnson. "Had you had a misunderstanding the day he died?" she asked, thinking how guilty Bev must feel if she'd been angry with him at the time of his death.

"Actually, no. We'd had a pleasant morning. I'd fixed him his favorite sausage and eggs."

Callie didn't know what to say to that. She changed the subject. "Why don't I go in Johnny's office and check it out so I can tell the cleaning people what to expect." Like bloodstains.

Beverly smiled gratefully. "That would be a help, Callie. No sense leaving that mess there like some kind of shrine."

"See, I knew there would be something I could do to help."

"I'll make us some tea."

Moments later Callie braced herself to open the office door. When she did, she was assailed with a sickening odor of dried blood, cigarette smoke, stale bourbon, and the unmistakable smell of fingerprinting powder. Virtually all of the prints found had been Johnny's, the police had said.

She opened the door a bit wider. The room looked much the same as it had in the crime-scene photos, minus the body. Johnny's blood had flooded onto the desk chair and dripped into a coagulated pool on the mat beneath it, but thankfully hadn't marred the carpet. The black fingerprinting powder was on everything, but she imagined it would wipe or vacuum up. As for the papers thrown willy-nilly all over the room, she could ask the cleaning service to stack them up for someone to go through and file later.

She was about to leave the suffocating room when she noticed the piece of tractor-feed paper extending from the printer. Curiously, she bent and looked at it. She remembered reading Beverly's statement, in which she'd said Johnny was working in his office when she and Tamra had left for the store. She'd known he was working because she'd heard the printer start up.

So this was what Johnny had been working on mere minutes before his death. A feed order, for alfalfa hay. Nothing sinister about that, except . . . the date. The order was dated October 3, a good week before Johnny's death.

Well, maybe he was printing up an extra copy for his files, Callie reasoned. He was such a meticulous man, he probably did everything in triplicate. It would be interesting to see if the order had been filled, though. She ripped off the paper, folded it into quarters, and stuck it in the back pocket of her jeans.

The door banged open and she whirled around, her hand going automatically to her throat in a gesture of fear.

Sam stood in the doorway, the devil's own fire burning in his eyes. "What the hell are you doing in *here*?"

SIX

"I . . . oh . . . you scared me," Callie said, her heart pounding.

"I guess so. What are you up to, Callie Calloway?"

She stared at Sam. "What do you *think* I'm up to?"

"Oh, just a little snooping around. Looking for clues at the scene of the crime, a crime that exists only in your imagination. Dreaming up headlines that would reinstate you at the *Record*, perhaps?"

She was so shocked by his anger, it took her a moment to find her voice. "You must really think I'm scum. For your information, I offered to call a cleaning service to take care of this room so no one in the family would have to. I was checking to see how bad it was, so I'd know what to tell the service when I call. I'm done, now." She didn't think she could stand another ten seconds in this room with its bloody reminder of the violence that had taken place. But Sam stood in her path like a stone monument.

"And you weren't looking to satisfy some morbid curiosity of your own?"

The piece of paper she'd torn from the printer burned in her back pocket. But she hadn't come into the room with the idea of snooping. She'd run across the feed order accidentally. Perhaps she shouldn't have removed it, but once she'd noted the anomaly, she had to follow up on it. She'd promised Sloan *and* Beverly.

Still, she didn't answer Sam's question directly. "If you think this is satisfying to me in some way, you're wrong. In fact . . ." Oh, dear. Bile rose in her throat. It was the smell. If she didn't get out of here soon, she was going to disgrace herself.

She tried to push past Sam. "Excuse me."

He grabbed her arm. "I'm not done talking to you."

"Talk to me outside!" She shook herself loose and bolted for the front door. Better to throw up in the bushes than on Beverly's living-room rug.

The moment the cool autumn air hit her she felt better. Leaning against the porch railing, she took in huge, gasping breaths, trying fruitlessly to wash the stench out of her nose.

"Callie?" Sam was right behind her with a steadying hand to her waist. "Good God, you turned green right before my eyes. Are you going to—"

"No," she said sharply. "I won't soil your shrubs." She was all right, now, feeling steadier by the moment. If only Sam would take his hand away.

Instead he moved closer. "Sure you're okay?"

"Fine."

He slipped his arm around her. "Come back inside. I heard Mom saying something about tea."

She stood rigid, glued to the spot. "I don't think so. I came by to check on you all, see if there was anything I could do to help. And, yes, I came to see you, because we have unfinished business." She was thinking about the explanation she owed him concerning her role in investigating his father's death.

But from the way he was looking at her, she guessed he was thinking about other unfinished business. "Do we?"

She sighed. The only way she was going to get this mess cleared up was to take the direct approach. She would be violating all sorts of confidences by what she was about to tell him, but she couldn't stand for this matter to hang between them any longer.

"The police suspect your father was murdered," she said. "Your mother believes the same thing, and I agree with them both. I'm working with the police on an informal basis because I happen to be close to the case. I promised I would let them know if anything useful turned up. I told your mother the same thing. That's the extent of my involvement. For the last time, I'm not planning to write any more stories about your father's death, for the *Record* or anyone else. If you don't believe me, I have nothing more to say to you."

During her speech, Sam had gradually pulled his arm away until they were no longer touching. Now he was silent. When Callie chanced a peek at him, she saw that his throat was working and his eyes glistened. "No one would kill him," he finally said, more to thin air than to Callie. "That's patently ridiculous. The case is closed."

"Officially it is. But not everyone agrees with that finding."

He turned to her suddenly. "So you're looking for some type of evidence that would reopen the case? To what purpose? So my family can be dragged through the mud some more?"

"Sam, if someone did kill your father, would you want that person to go free?"

"No, of course not."

"Neither do I."

"But there *is* no such person." He said this as if the forcefulness of his words could make it so.

"I want to be sure of that," Callie said quietly. "The media will never know about this unless something concrete does turn up, and then only if someone at the *Record* is astute enough to figure it out. You'll have to trust me on that."

"I guess I don't have a choice." He sighed and relaxed a fractional degree. "I don't agree with what you're doing, though. The sooner Mom accepts the truth that Dad killed himself, the sooner she can get over it. You're not helping by encouraging her to live in this la-la land of plots and murders."

"I'm doing what I believe is right." That was all she could offer him.

"Fine." He paused, then said gruffly, "Come back inside. Have some tea. Spend time with my mother. You always do her a world of good."

"But I don't seem to be of much help to you. Every time I turn around I'm making you mad."

"That's just me, I guess. I think I'm not quite ready to be comforted."

The pain in his eyes moved her. Everyone expected Sam to be the strong one, the one in control. He'd been the backbone of the family for a long time. He'd probably been so busy taking care of everything after Johnny's death that he hadn't had time to grieve.

"If there's ever anything I can do—"

He looked at her sharply, cutting off her words. The pain in his eyes receded, replaced by something else—raw need. Suddenly she knew what she could do, how she could connect to this man who usually seemed to demand so little in the way of emotional support.

She felt it, too, an answering need inside her. Right there on his front porch, an understanding passed between them that went beyond anything they'd experienced together.

He looked away first. She took a deep breath, wondering if she'd imagined the whole thing. Maybe she had. But she couldn't escape the nagging feeling that a bargain had been struck.

Callie spent the next two days in a state of perpetual near hysteria. Without a single word, she'd practically issued an engraved invitation to Sam. She'd been positive that, for once, they'd been on the same wavelength. If they hadn't been on his mother's front porch—if they'd been somewhere more private—her fate would have been sealed then and there.

Maybe Sam had thought better of the whole idea. At any rate, she'd been given a reprieve. She was tempted to pack her bags and run away until Sam was gone and things were safe in Destiny.

She managed to forget about Sam for a few minutes Tuesday morning as she worked in the garden belonging to her landlord—the man who lived in the "big house" to which her carriage house was attached. He was out of town and had told her to make use of anything she could scavenge there among the autumn-shriveled plants.

She wasn't much for gardens, but she was on a strict budget now and couldn't afford to turn down free food. So here she was, wearing her oldest jeans and a long-sleeved T-shirt that dated from college, gathering tomatoes and peppers and one rather sickly looking butternut squash.

When she was finished, she turned the hose on, hoping to keep the plants alive a few more days or weeks, until that first freeze.

She brought her treasures inside and dumped them into the sink to be washed.

The phone rang and her heart jumped. Never had the phone attained such significance in her life. She should have been hoping, praying, the call was from one of the newspapers she'd applied to. Instead she thought of Sam.

"Hello?" She tried to make her voice sound normal.

The caller was neither Sam nor a newspaper. It was Sandler's Feed Store. "This is Wayne Pedder, Ms. Calloway. You said you had a question about Johnny Sanger's account?"

Callie took a deep breath. "Yessir." She rummaged around on her cluttered counter until she located the wrinkled feed order she'd snagged from Johnny's printer. "Johnny ordered some alfalfa hay on October third, is that correct?"

"Yes, ma'am."

"And was the hay delivered?"

"Oh, yes, ma'am, the very next day. Is there a problem?"

"No, not at all. I was just curious about something. How did he place the order? Did he call?"

"No, ma'am, he always faxes in his orders. We've gone tech-no-logical around here," Wayne said proudly. "He pays with a credit-card number, and we deliver a receipt with the hay. Johnny Sanger thought up the system. Saves a lot of time and paperwork."

"I see." So maybe Johnny had simply printed up a hard copy for his files. That would make sense, even a week after the fact.

"Anything else, Ms. Calloway? Do you need me to spell my name?"

"Oh, um, I'm not doing a story for the paper," she admitted. "Just tying up a few loose ends."

"Oh." He sounded supremely disappointed.

She concluded the conversation, then ran back downstairs to turn off the water. She was disappointed herself. She'd thought maybe the feed order would be an important clue.

"Silly," she murmured to herself. If it had been important, the police would have done something about it. Come to think of it, they'd probably already checked it out.

She turned purposefully toward the carriage house—and almost had a collision with Sam. Oh, terrific! She hadn't even had a shower yet this morning.

"What are you doing here?" she demanded, rather ungraciously, she realized, after the words were out. Of course, he looked freshly showered, his caramel-and-gold hair still slightly damp, his jaw smooth.

"Is that any way to treat a man who's brought you kolaches?"

"Kolaches?" she repeated, inhaling to catch the scent of her favorite pastry.

He held up a white bakery bag. "Don't tell me you've already eaten."

"No . . ."

"Something wrong?"

"You couldn't have called first?"

"I did. No answer. You can check your answering machine," he added when she started to object. "You were probably out here playing Mary, Mary, Quite Contrary."

No, more like Cinderella before the fairy godmother got to her, she thought, eyeing the grime on her hands. Where was a fairy godmother when you needed one?

Callie considered telling him to go away and come back later, when she was presentable. But then she looked at the bakery bag, thought about her recently enacted policy of not turning down free food, and decided she'd be smarter not to leave Sam and the bag alone together for too much longer.

"Well, it was nice of you to think of me." She pasted on a smile she hoped would hide her sudden case of nerves. For heaven's sake, this was Sam! He'd seen her in worse states than this. What was there to be nervous about?

Oh, nothing, only the fact that she'd implied a certain promise, and that's why he was here bearing gifts.

"I'll finish watering here," he said, "if you'd like a chance to, um, freshen up?"

She couldn't very well deny that she needed some heavy-duty freshening. "I'm done watering. You can come upstairs and warm these in the oven while I jump in the shower." She turned and walked sedately, trying her best to hide her inner turmoil. Was he really here, without Deana, for the reason she thought?

She showered quickly with her strawberry-scented soap, dusted herself with the bath powder she hadn't used in years, and put on the only pair of matching panties and bra she had—purple silk. She thought about Sam's bold gaze taking in the sexy lingerie, his hands unfastening the front clasp of the bra and sliding the silk panties over her hips and down.

She shivered. There wasn't a single doubt in her mind that her vision could become reality.

When at last she felt ready, dressed in purple jeans and a thin lilac sweater, her damp hair braided, she entered the kitchen. The coffee she'd put on to brew earlier was ready, and Sam had popped the kolaches into the oven to warm.

"They'll be ready in about five minutes," he said. His gaze lingered on her for several long seconds. "You look nice."

Nice? Was that the best he could come up with? She laughed at herself. This was Sam, who had never been a man of many words. "Thanks." She brushed dangerously close to him on the way to the coffeepot. She fancied she could hear a sharp intake of breath as she passed, but maybe that was only her overactive imagination.

She filled two pale blue ceramic mugs she'd bought last spring from Millicent at a crafts fair. She'd been waiting for the perfect opportunity to use them, and this was definitely it.

"So, what's the occasion?" she asked with feigned naïveté as she set mugs, plates, and napkins on the small round table in her breakfast nook. "You don't often bribe me with Polish pastries without a reason."

"No occasion," Sam said, also pretending innocence. "Mom wanted to take Deana shopping, and I thought it would be a good time to visit with . . . a friend."

Friend? Had she misread him? Was this merely a gesture of apology for his unfounded accusations of the other day? But when she looked into his eyes, the utter sincerity she saw there took her by surprise. The air crackled with electricity as they stared at each other with possibilities brimming between them.

"No, more than a friend," he said, his voice husky. "I mean it. I've never been in love with anyone else, not even my wife. I'm ashamed to say I married a woman I didn't love, but at the time I thought affection would grow into love. It didn't. Because every time I looked at her, I thought of you and wished you were there instead. Even if she'd halfway tried to be a good wife, poor Debra didn't stand a chance."

Callie was too stunned to speak for a moment. She'd expected a sexual overture. She hadn't expected this abrupt outpouring from Sam, which had sounded something like a rehearsed speech. He so seldom talked about his feelings. Back when they were dating, he'd mentioned that he loved her maybe a couple of times, one of those being when he'd proposed marriage.

"Do you love me now?" she asked, her voice quavering. She hadn't anticipated things getting this heavy this fast. She felt ill prepared to deal with it. She hadn't analyzed her own feelings for Sam or tried to separate nostalgia and remembered emotions from the here and now, the real thing. All she'd known was that she wanted to be with him, whatever the circumstances.

He shrugged helplessly. "I'm still getting acquainted with the woman you've become, Callie. But I'm pretty sure that if I were given half a chance, I'd fall in love with you all over again, even if it wasn't the smartest thing to do."

"Oh, Sam, I . . ." Words simply failed her. Her throat tightened, and tears of some very strong emotion threatened to spill from her eyes.

Sam went to her then and put his arms around her, holding her as gently as he would a fragile bird or priceless porcelain. "Don't cry, darlin'," he said, rubbing her back.

She settled against him, listening to the soothing, steady beat of his heart. The familiarity of his embrace was like a balm to her soul. It was almost like they'd never been apart.

The oven timer went off. Sam reached over and silenced it, then turned off the oven. "Callie?"

"Mmm."

"Unless you stop me, I'm going to pick you up and carry you into the bedroom and have my way with you."

"I won't stop you," she said, her words muffled

against his chest. Her soul ached for completion. For years she'd felt as if she and Sam were a book with the last page unread. It was time. "Let's finish what we started all those years ago."

He swung her into his arms with almost no struggle. "We're not finishing anything. I prefer to think of it as a start of something even bigger."

Callie didn't have the heart to argue with him. She threw her arms around his neck and kissed him, hard. In five swift strides he'd reached the bedroom. The door was slightly ajar and he elbowed it open and walked in like he owned the place.

He broke the kiss. Breathing heavily, he laid her on the twin bed, eyeing its small confines dubiously.

"It's a tiny bedroom," she said, reading his thoughts. "I didn't need a larger bed."

Sam sat on the edge of the bed and pulled off his boots. "You don't do a lot of entertaining, then?"

"Sam, what a question! Of course not. This is Destiny, Texas, remember? You don't sleep around in Destiny unless you want everyone to think you're a floozy."

He grabbed her by the ankle and pulled off one of her purple socks, then ran his thumbnail along the sole of her foot.

A delicious shiver worked its way up her spine.

"So you've never . . ."

"I said 'not a lot,'" she quipped. She was no sex goddess, but surely he didn't think she was a virgin.

He pulled off her other sock, then leaned across her, covering her body with his until he was face-to-face with her. His breath smelled like sweet coffee. "I wish I'd been your first. I sure wanted to be."

"I wish that too," she said. "I'm sorry I was such a prude."

He smiled faintly. "You had strong convictions, and good reasons behind them. I respected you for that, even when I was a raging mass of hormones. I never thought you were a prude."

"Thank you, Sam." Somehow, that little bit of understanding about the person she was back then made Callie feel warm all over. "Do we have to talk about it anymore?" She was afraid they might talk themselves out of doing something they knew was a little bit foolish.

"Talk is cheap." He nipped her earlobe. "I think of myself as a man of action."

Oh, and such action! Callie closed her eyes, forgot her doubts, and let Sam's hands and mouth and tongue take her to wonderful places she remembered as well as places she'd never been. He took his time, kissing her mouth, her jaw, then her collarbone above her scoop neckline. His fingertips skimmed over the softness of the lilac sweater, lingering on her breasts, then skittered under the hem.

Callie's stomach muscles tightened at that first innocent contact of his hand on her bare skin. She pulled his head against her face and inhaled deeply. Ah, he still washed his hair with baby shampoo. Funny how those little details of his life, things she'd taken for granted when they were kids, could seem so intimate, now. Like knowing the brands of shampoo and shaving cream he preferred.

And the underwear . . . Hanes cotton briefs. Always white.

Suddenly she had to know. His belt buckle was pressing against her hipbone anyway. She wiggled until he raised up, a questioning look on his face. He was lying half on, half off her, and she slid out from underneath.

"Callie?"

She reached for his belt buckle, nudging him over on his back. "Take off those jeans, cowboy." She whipped off the belt with one hard yank.

His curious expression changed to one of pure predatory mischief. "Only if you take yours off." He smiled wickedly. "Or I'll take 'em off for you." His hand darted out, quick as a cobra, and caught her belt loop.

She laughed and tried to escape, but he was too fast and too strong. In moments he had her back down on the bed, and the battle was on to see who could get whom undressed the fastest.

He pushed her sweater above her breasts, chuckling and muttering something about "color-coordinated wardrobes."

She pulled out the shirttail of his Western shirt, then unsnapped and unzipped his Wranglers, revealing the white briefs. She murmured something about his predictability, which he didn't understand but obviously didn't care about.

He pulled the sweater over her head and went to work on her bra, unfastening the front clasp with his teeth.

"Show-off!" she objected, giggling at his audacity. Then she reached inside his jeans and wrapped her hand around his erection, paralyzing him momentarily. He groaned and his body went limp—well, most of it.

"No fair," he said, breathing hard.

"All's fair in love and war." She released him and shrugged out of the bra. His eyes, burning with blue fire, feasted on her bareness. His hand followed his gaze, cupping one breast and rubbing the rosy nipple with his thumb.

Now it was her turn to groan. Tears of pure, unadulterated joy threatened, but she savagely swallowed them back. She'd forgotten how good he could make her feel with so little.

The contest was over. She stepped away from him just long enough to unfasten her jeans and shimmy out of them. His eyes followed her every move, hungry, impatient.

She didn't make him wait long. Naked, aching for more of his touch, she helped him pull off his jeans, briefs, socks, and then draped herself over him, allowing his erection to settle between her thighs, poised at her entrance.

He throbbed with his need for her; she vibrated with passion, her eager flesh moving with him, seeking the most advantageous contact, the most thrilling caress. She felt every square inch where they touched, from his roughly haired legs against her smooth ones, to his hard chest against her soft breasts, to his freshly shaven cheek against her lips. His hands, at once rough and gentle, massaged her buttocks and thighs.

She spread her legs a little farther, adjusting herself, holding her breath against that first sensual invasion she knew was only seconds away.

His eyes glazed over for a split second when she lowered herself over his tip. But the man of action quickly returned, encircling her waist with his hands and assuming control. He lowered her the rest of the way with infinite slowness, causing her to shudder with the exquisite, ever-changing sensations. When he had filled her completely, he released her and, without moving, just looked at her.

The tears that had threatened earlier returned, and she couldn't stop them this time.

Somehow, instinctively maybe, he knew her tears were joyful ones. He wiped one off her cheek, then licked the moisture from his finger, as if he wanted to share everything, every nuance of this moment, with her.

She'd dreamed about it so often, even when he was married, even when she thought there was no chance it would ever really happen. But none of her fantasies had prepared her for the absolute perfection of this moment. She wanted to trap it, hold it, but it was, after all, a single moment.

He began to move inside her. Quickly caught up in the new sensations, she didn't waste any energy mourning the passage of time. She coordinated her movements with his, rocking back and forth as he thrust upward, sheathing and unsheathing his hardness within her slick, wet depths.

It was paradise, and it was over too quickly. She dug her fingers into the firm flesh of his shoulders as the sensations built to a crescendo, a crashing waterfall of warmth and light that made all other climaxes pale by comparison. She collapsed against him, still convulsing with waves and flickers of pleasure. He thrust several more times, his groans of pleasure escalating until he cried out with one, magnificent push.

Her heart soared with his for a few moments. And then they were once again earthbound, two glistening bodies in her tiny twin bed, still on top of the covers. They were once again Callie and Sam, but not the same two people who had entered the room a few minutes earlier.

They remained joined for a long time. Callie savored the intimate coupling, but eventually her legs started to quiver and the position became uncomfortable, so she slid away from him. He made a mild, token protest against the inevitable, then snuggled her against his shoulder, his hand lightly caressing her abdomen.

"Do you—" Callie stopped, surprised at the way her voice had shattered the silence.

"What?"

"Um, do you think it would have been this way if we'd made love before?" She knew Sam would know what she meant by *this way*. Their lovemaking had been unquestioningly spectacular, and if he denied it he was a liar.

Of course he didn't deny it. "I don't think it would have been the same. We were young and inexperienced and frightened."

"Then I'm glad we waited. Does that seem stupid?" She played with the curly gold hair on his chest.

"No."

They were silent for a long time. Callie listened to him breathe. Sparrows were chirping outside, and late-morning sunlight filtered in through her gauze curtains, making patterns on the bed and on their naked bodies. Yup, this was just about as perfect an existence as anyone could wish for. Afterglow.

"There's another reason I came here today, Callie," Sam said after a while.

Uh-oh. Somehow, Callie got this feeling that the other shoe was about to drop. "And what reason was that?" Instinctively she clung more tightly to him.

"I'm already late getting fall roundup going. I have to return to the ranch."

"Oh . . . when?" She tried not to sound as devastated as she felt. She had, after all, known what the game plan was from the very beginning. She just hadn't imagined she'd be losing him so soon.

"Tomorrow."

"Tomorrow?" A panicky feeling whirled in her stomach.

"I can't delay it. Mom's situation is pretty stable right now. We're waiting on lawyers and such to settle the will and do all the probate stuff. I've asked her to come back to Nevada with me and she's accepted. A change of scenery will do her good."

"What about the farm?"

"Will volunteered to look after things. He's working nights at the recycling plant." Sam paused. "Amazing how he's turned around in the past few months. I think Tamra's had a good effect on him."

Callie kept her opinions about Will to herself. "I don't want you to go so soon," she said, hating to sound so needy. But she had to tell him what she was feeling.

"I don't want to go at all. But . . ."

"I know. You have to." Just like he'd had to go help

his uncle when he was younger. When she was a girl, his willingness to abandon her had hurt. It still did. But at least now she could understand it. Of course he had to go back, if there were problems at Roundrock. The ranch in Nevada was his livelihood. In addition to his own living, he employed several people who depended on him.

She fought the desire to argue with him.

"You could come with me," he said, quietly, calmly.

SEVEN

"What?" That was the last thing she'd expected to hear from him.

"Well, what better time for a visit? I've asked you a million times over the years to come to Nevada with me to see why I could never give up the ranch, but you always had something more important—"

"Yeah, like a job, or school," she shot back. "Surely you didn't expect me to—"

"Easy, Callie," he interrupted before she worked up a full head of steam. "Back then, maybe I did expect you to drop everything and follow me regardless of your situation. What can I say? I was a self-centered kid, like most boys that age. But this is different. You're between jobs. What do you have holding you here right now?"

What he said made perfect sense. What was more, it held undeniable appeal. She'd never seen a real ranch before, not a huge spread like Roundrock. But she couldn't help digging in her heels. What was she afraid of? That she would like it? That she would want to stay?

That he would talk her into marrying him and giving up her journalism career?

She gave a mental snort. It wasn't as if Sam was asking her to stay, she reminded herself. He'd said "a visit." A week or two, maybe. After his disastrous marriage, he'd think long and hard before offering himself as a husband to a city girl. She didn't think she had anything to worry about in that department.

"My mother really wants you to come," Sam said.

Suddenly she felt like she'd missed too many opportunities over the years. She wanted to grab things when they came along, rather than waiting around.

One will tarry, losing her chance at love. Theodora's words came back to haunt her. Well, she wasn't tarrying anymore.

"Okay." It was for Beverly, Callie told herself. She wanted to be there for her friend, if she was needed.

"Okay?"

She smiled and rolled onto her side to face him, still in the protective circle of his arm. "I'll argue some more if you want."

"No," he said, chuckling. "I just expected more of a fight."

"We used to always argue for the sake of arguing. I hope we've gotten over that."

"Me too. We have enough real differences without making up more."

Callie, not normally an early riser, found her eyes wide open at five A.M. her first morning at Roundrock. They'd arrived late the night before after an all-day journey by car, plane, and car again. She'd been so exhausted she'd fallen onto the bed in her street clothes, instantly asleep.

But now she felt completely rested and oddly peaceful.

She slid out of bed and stripped down, anxious to get a look at this place that claimed so much of Sam's devotion. Roundrock represented the future she'd been offered but had refused. What if she discovered she had made the wrong decision? Or, she thought with a twinge of unease, what if Sam regretted inviting her to Nevada? He'd issued the invitation on impulse, while they'd lain naked together in her bed enjoying the afterglow of lovemaking. He might actually be reluctant to share this part of his life with an outsider, which she definitely was.

The room had grown chilly during the night, and she quickly located a robe from her suitcase and wrapped it around her. A nice, hot shower was what she needed, and then, if no one was up yet, she'd wander downstairs to the kitchen and see about coffee. She was sure Sam wouldn't mind her making herself at home.

She tiptoed into the hallway, immediately intimidated by the sheer number of doors, all of them closed. Sam had shown her last night where the bathroom was, but she'd been half-asleep.

The first door she tried was to the nursery. Deana was asleep in a tangle of covers, her tousled blond curls all that was visible. The tiny lump under the blankets rose and fell reassuringly, however. A blazing bedside lamp was testament to the fact that Deana hadn't conquered her fear of the dark.

"Neither have I, kiddo," she murmured, resisting the urge to go to the bed and stroke those pretty blond curls. If Deana suddenly awakened, though, and needed a diaper change or food or something, Callie would be at a loss.

She quietly withdrew and tried another door. This one led into a darkened room. Callie opened it wider to admit light from the hall. Immediately she knew this wasn't a bathroom, either, but she didn't close the door right away.

This was Sam's room, and Callie's eyes focused on the softly snoring form in the middle of a king-size bed. She was drawn to him, even more strongly than his daughter had drawn her. Only the fear of what he would think if he woke up kept her feet glued to the floor.

Eventually she persuaded herself to back out and make a quiet, dignified exit.

The next door she tried was indeed a bathroom, with old-fashioned hexagonal tiles in black-and-white blocks, and a huge footed tub. What a temptation!

But not this morning. Someone else might be needing the bathroom; she couldn't hog it for a leisurely bath. She took a quick shower in water that was only lukewarm no matter how she adjusted the faucets, brushed her teeth, and returned to her room to dress in jeans and a sweater.

It took Callie several minutes to find the kitchen. She was astounded at the vastness of the ranch house. Sam had described it to her, but he'd never conveyed the true size of the place. Her whole apartment would easily fit in the central living area that surrounded a stone fireplace. She blundered into a formal living room furnished with Early American antiques, an office, and another dining hall with a table that would seat a dozen people. Finally, following the scent of coffee, she found the enormous, old-fashioned kitchen.

Beverly was already there, watching the oversized percolator as it did its thing.

"You couldn't sleep?" Callie asked, concerned for Beverly, who had developed dark shadows under her eyes over the past couple of weeks.

"Actually, I slept quite well last night, better than any night since Johnny . . . left me. I'm just an early riser. Comes from being raised on a ranch, I guess."

"Oh, that's right, this is where you grew up. I forget that, sometimes."

"And I couldn't wait to get away," Beverly said with a fond smile. "My first husband and I ran off and got married against my father's wishes. We were set on moving to the city and living in the fast lane."

"Sounds kind of romantic." Callie joined Beverly in her vigil over the slow coffeepot.

"It might've sounded that way, but it wasn't, especially when he left me, pregnant and destitute. Thank God I met Johnny."

"Did you come back here?" Callie asked.

"No. My uncle Ned would have found a place for Johnny. But Johnny didn't want anything handed to him. He wanted his own spread." She paused, a faraway look on her face. "Oddly, I don't regret turning my back on Roundrock. Our little place never quite fulfilled the dreams Johnny had for it, but we were happy most of the time." She sighed. "Oh, dear, I hope I don't get all weepy again."

Callie touched Beverly's hand in silent commiseration. She thought about Nicole, wondering again how the Johnny Sanger she'd known could have been unfaithful to his wife. He'd been a man of high principles, loyal, a family man. He wouldn't have done anything to hurt Beverly.

Maybe he hadn't had an affair with Nicole. Maybe there was a perfectly logical explanation for his association with her. Callie felt an urge to ask Beverly if she knew.

Fortunately, a timely interruption prevented her from saying anything unforgivably stupid. Rena arrived. Rena, Roundrock's cook, housekeeper, and all-around boss woman, was legendary. Callie had been hearing about her for years. But, like the house, no descriptions had prepared Callie for the real thing.

"Here, now, who's messing with my coffeepot?" were the first words out of her mouth. She was tiny—probably under five feet, Callie guessed—and dressed in faded bell-bottom jeans and a yellow flannel shirt. Her black-and-silver-streaked hair was pulled back in a braid so tight that it stretched the flesh of Rena's wizened brown face. Her eyes, darting around accusingly, were dark brown or black and sharp as a crow's.

"It's just me, Rena," Beverly said, unruffled by the attack. "I always did beat you to the kitchen."

Rena's suspicious expression immediately softened. "Why, Beverly, it *is* you. Sorry to hear about your old man."

Beverly nodded.

Rena focused her raisin eyes on Callie. "Who are you?"

Beverly answered. "This is Sam's friend Callie. She's been a great help to us."

Rena's thin eyebrows flew up. "Sam's Callie, you say? The same one?"

"Same one," Beverly confirmed while Callie, tongue-tied for once, endured Rena's examination. Apparently she didn't pass inspection, because the old woman eventually shrugged and looked away without a single word of greeting or welcome.

"I'm late getting breakfast started," she groused. "You all git your coffee and clear out. Give me some room."

Before they could follow orders, Sam entered the kitchen. He looked better than ever in his battered work clothes, Callie thought, suppressing a lascivious grin. The worn-to-white denim of his tight-fitting jeans intimately cupped his anatomy in a way that made Callie blush. She focused on his face, his damp hair combed back from his forehead, his hat—not the dress Stetson he'd worn in Destiny, but a battered old straw thing that looked more like a bird's nest than a hat—dangling from his hand.

She'd seen the man a million times, but her heart lurched anyway, as if for a long-lost lover.

"Oh, great," Rena said, "now the boss is up early. I suppose that means the young 'un is up too?"

"Not yet," Sam said. "She had a late night last night."

"I'll take care of her while I'm here, Rena," Beverly

offered. "It'll give me something to do, keep my mind off . . . things."

Sam spared a smile of encouragement for his mother, then turned back to Rena. "We're in a hurry this morning. Something we can carry with us would be good."

"Great. Guess that does in my idea of flapjacks. All of you—out!"

"Yes, ma'am," Sam said with a fond smile for the woman who, Callie knew, was dear to him as his own grandmother.

In the dining hall, some of the other cowboys were drifting in. Sam made cursory introductions, explaining that most of them were neighbors and temporary help brought in to assist with fall roundup. Rena brought in a pot of coffee and a tray of cups.

"So what are you in such a hurry for this morning?" Callie asked, finding a battered chair. "Is there a big problem, or is this just routine stuff?"

"Little of both," he answered, seeming pleased that she was showing an interest. "A neighboring ranch has reported an outbreak of pleuropneumonia. I want to make double sure all of our calves are vaccinated against it. An epidemic could kill off an entire year's calves."

"Oh, Sam!" Beverly said. "That's scary. When I was a little girl, we had some kind of epidemic like that."

Sam grimaced. "Yeah, it's nothing to take lightly. Fortunately, we have the vaccines. We're also working against a deadline, though. Cold weather's on the way, and I'd rather not get caught by a freak snowstorm with a bunch of heifers and calves up in the high country."

"I tried to get Bud Vinson and his copter, but he's

got other work lined up," said Mitch Dalton, the foreman. Callie had met him the night before, when he'd
picked them up at the airport. He'd seemed friendly
enough, but his eyes were full of suspicion as he slid a
sideways glance at her now and then. Did everybody
here know about her past with Sam?

"That's okay," Sam said. "We've got Punky on our
side. Best damn cow dog you ever saw." Sam glanced at
Callie. The brag was definitely meant for her benefit.

Callie felt very much like an outsider. Everyone here
was speaking a foreign language. Well, not foreign, exactly. She could understand it. But she couldn't contribute, not a word. She felt ignorant.

Suddenly she was seized with a keen desire to learn
about Roundrock. She could do a feature story on
it—yes, it was a brilliant idea! City-slicker girl learns to
rope and ride in two short weeks, stepping in to help a
ranch avoid a pleuro-whatever epidemic. She could ped-
dle that concept to any number of magazines.

"I want to go with you." The words popped out of
her mouth.

"What?" Sam looked at her like she'd grown a third
arm.

"I want to see what you're doing, and maybe I could
find a way to help you."

The other cowboys burst into laughter, and even
Beverly smiled, but Sam just stared. "Callie, you've
never even ridden a horse." This elicited another round
of laughter from the cowboys.

"I'm a quick learner. Mostly I imagine you just have
to stick in the saddle and let the horse do all the work."

The laughter turned to hysterics. Callie's face burned. She would curl up and die if Sam ridiculed her.

He didn't, though. The look he gave her was gentle, if a little condescending. "Callie, I'm happy that you want to learn about the ranch. And I promise I'll teach you anything you want to know—but not for the next couple of days. Today is going to be tough enough without my having to worry about you falling off a horse and breaking your neck."

He was right, of course, and Callie nodded reluctantly. Still, the idea for the story burned inside her.

Rena returned to the dining hall in record time with a huge platter filled with biscuit sandwiches—egg, cheese, and sausage. Callie couldn't imagine how the cook had produced all that food so quickly. She decided Rena's role at the ranch would make a wonderful sidebar to the story.

The cowboys grabbed for the breakfast sandwiches, devouring them in one or two bites. They wrapped extras in paper napkins and stuffed them in their jacket pockets. The whole process took about thirty seconds, and they began clearing out.

"My, they are in a hurry," Callie said, taking a tentative bite of a biscuit. It was heavenly. She decided not to think about fat grams while she was here.

"I have to go," Sam said reluctantly. "Sorry I can't—"

"It's okay, Sam. Really, I don't expect you to babysit me while I'm here. I'm resourceful enough to keep busy."

He smiled. "Still . . ." He looked around. His mother was paying rapt attention to her breakfast. "Let me show you something real quick." He led Callie out of the dining hall and into the deserted living room, where he wasted no time pulling her into his arms and kissing the stuffing out of her.

Her thirsty soul responded, soaking up his affection like the cracked ground in a drought soaks up rain. She met his tongue with hers, surprised, excited, and a little intimidated by the strength of Sam's passion.

Abruptly he broke away. "Welcome to Roundrock," he said with a mischievous wink. "Make yourself at home. I'll be back for dinner." He kissed her again before she could even say anything. "Mmm, wish it could be more." He released her and walked away to join his men.

Callie touched her lips, not sure whether she should smile or frown. The kiss had awakened her better than even the caffeine-laden coffee had, and she knew she would think of it often during the day. She was also sure that's what Sam had intended.

But she chafed at the role of the "little woman" waiting at home for her man to return from his manly work.

Well, it was only a temporary situation, she told herself as she wandered back into the dining hall to finish her biscuit and coffee. Anyway, she had plenty to occupy herself for today, or even a few days, until Sam had time to teach her about ranching.

Funny, she'd never imagined herself wanting to learn something like that.

❖———❖

Callie thought she had plenty to keep her busy. First she called home and checked her answering machine. Nothing.

Next she called Sloan. She felt guilty for walking away from the mystery of Johnny Sanger's death and leaving Sloan to his own devices. She'd promised to help, and now she'd bugged out. She wanted to let him know that she was still keeping her eyes and ears open, even up here in Nevada. And she was still thinking.

"Have you questioned Nicole Johnson?" she asked Sloan at the first opportunity. Not that he owed her any explanations.

"Danny Fowler did. I sat in. Uh, I don't think she did it, Callie."

"Oh, I don't either," Callie said quickly. "Her grief was too genuine. But that doesn't mean she isn't involved somehow. If she was . . . spending time with Johnny, he might have confided in her."

"Exactly. And she is hiding something. I just don't know what." He sighed. "Nicole *isn't* a bad person. I've known her for years. And, for your information, I don't believe she and Johnny were physically involved. I think they were friends, just like she claims."

Callie didn't say anything. She was unutterably relieved to hear someone echo her own thoughts.

"Pretty naive of me, huh?" Sloan said.

"No. Not at all. Did Johnny actually leave her anything in his will? She seemed to believe he would."

"Maybe he would have, if he'd known he was going to die. We'll never know."

Callie ended the conversation by promising Sloan that she'd let him know if either Sam or Beverly told her anything useful, tamping down the twinge of guilt she felt over "spying" on her friends.

Putting Johnny's death out of her mind once more, Callie sent out her daily round of résumés. The quarter-mile walk down to the mailbox allowed her her first good look at Roundrock. It was picture-postcard impressive. The view went on for miles, and she wondered how much of what she could see was Sanger land.

She stood and looked at the view, with its subtle colors of green-and-purple sagebrush across the valley the ranch was nestled in. A thin mist shrouded mountain slopes in the distance. The scene's subtle paint-box hues wavered and changed as the sun played hide-and-seek behind wispy clouds. She hadn't imagined that Nevada would be so colorful. The air was crisp and cold too. Frost still clung to the tan grass in shady areas. But it was a dry, invigorating chill that made Callie want to run laps—or maybe even ride a horse.

When she returned to the house, she wandered into the kitchen, where Rena was baking.

Rena gruffly refused Callie's offer of help. So Callie poured herself another cup of coffee, as if she weren't wired enough already, and sat down at the table where Rena was rolling out dough.

"Are you making pie?" Callie asked.

"Mm-hmm."

"What kind?"

"Blueberry."

Callie's mouth watered. "You've been with Sam's family a long time, I guess. I remember Sam talking about you when he was just a kid."

"Mm-hmm."

Her answers didn't invite further questions, so Callie quieted down for a while. She suspected Rena would be even more reticent if she learned Callie was thinking of writing a story about Roundrock.

Callie decided to ask questions of a less personal nature. "How big is Babcock?"

"Dunno. A few hundred people, I guess."

"Does it have a newspaper?"

Rena finally cracked a smile, but it wasn't a kind one. "What would we need a newspaper for? Nothing ever happens."

Callie didn't argue, but she knew differently. Most people were hungry for news of their community, no matter how small.

It was easy to see why Sam's wife had gone stir-crazy here. Not that that was any excuse for leaving a husband and baby, but Callie could sympathize with the boredom. She looked forward to the time when Sam would be free to show her around and teach her to ride. If she was going to fit in around here, even for two weeks, she would have to find some useful pursuit.

"What do the men do for lunch?" she asked Rena.

"I'll take it to them."

"Oh, do you need some help?" She couldn't keep the eagerness out of her voice. It was pathetic, how desperate she was for a few minutes with Sam.

"Not really."

"But I'd like to help." Then she could find out what Sam and his men were doing. She'd come here for him, not his empty ranch house.

Rena sighed. "You can come along if you're really that bored."

"Thank you," Callie replied. "Just call out when you're ready. I'll be in the house somewhere."

She wandered around for a bit, eventually stumbling on Beverly in the living room, reading a story to Deana, both of them tucked under an afghan. Beverly looked up, and Deana jumped off the couch, running like a steer out of the shoot at a rodeo. She wrapped her chubby arms around Callie's legs. "Callll," she said in obvious delight.

Callie picked her up. She was amazed at how comfortable she was starting to feel with the little girl. "Hi, munchkin."

Beverly smiled. "I guess I haven't been very good company this morning, Callie. You must be bored stiff."

"Not really. I'm going with Rena to take lunch to the men."

"Oh? Are you sure you want to do that? They're up to some messy, disgusting work, you know."

"I want to see it. I'm not sure why I have this sudden urge to learn about Sam's ranch—"

"I think I know." Beverly said with quiet certainty.

Callie could guess what Beverly was thinking, and she quickly shook her head. "It's not because I want to live here. I just never realized the ranch would be so . . . intriguing. I'm thinking of writing some kind of story about it—that is, if you and Sam don't object."

"Doesn't bother me," Beverly said complacently.

"Good. Um, since I have a few minutes, there's something I want to ask you." She thought briefly of Nicole, then nixed the idea again. Not in front of Deana. Maybe never. "It's about Johnny and his computer. He was pretty proud of it, huh?"

Beverly smiled nostalgically. "He thought getting computerized was the best thing to come along since sliced bread. He's always hated paperwork, and the computer saved him a lot."

"I understand that he used a fax modem to place orders for feed."

"And for any other supplies we needed. Almost every business has a fax machine these days."

"And then did he print a hard copy of the fax for himself, for the files?"

Beverly looked surprised. "Oh, heavens, no. He didn't believe in making hard copies of anything. A receipt for the goods was all the paperwork he needed." Beverly narrowed her gaze. "Why are you asking me about this?"

"Because . . ." She took a deep breath. "The last thing Johnny printed before he died was a hard copy of a week-old feed order."

"You mean, when I heard the printer . . ."

Callie nodded. "It might not mean anything, Bev," she cautioned. "If he was distraught, he could have simply pushed the wrong button."

"But then, what did he intend to print?"

The question hung between them.

"Callie!" Rena's voice boomed from the kitchen. "We're leaving in five minutes!"

"You better run along," Beverly said. "Rena won't hesitate to go without you."

Callie gave Beverly a quick hug, almost squashing Deana between them. But she didn't go right to the kitchen. She wanted to talk to Sloan about her newest suspicion. She ran upstairs and punched in his number on the extension in her room. But he wasn't available, so she was forced to leave a message.

Her five minutes were slipping away fast. She ran full tilt for the kitchen.

"There." Rena, pointed to a box.

Callie grabbed the box off the table and breathed in the scent of freshly baked corn bread and steaming chili as she followed Rena out the back door to her battered pickup truck. The sun had chased the nip from the air, and Callie found she didn't even need a jacket.

"Beautiful day," she said to the reticent Rena as they both climbed into the cab of the truck.

"Warm for October," Rena offered.

The truck bounced its way along dirt roads that crisscrossed acres and acres of pastureland. Some pastures were empty, some contained placidly grazing cattle, many of them with half-grown calves nearby.

When they finally located the cowboys, the scene wasn't exactly what Callie had pictured. No one was on a horse. In fact, all the horses were tethered nearby, looking bored as they cropped browning grass. The action was in some pens, which looked as if they'd been hastily built that morning. Groups of white-faced cattle were milling about nervously. The men were gathered in two small groups, doing something to the animals.

Rena rang a bell, announcing lunch's arrival. "Come and git it while it's hot!" she bellowed.

Callie's gaze locked onto Sam. He was sweaty and dusty—and was that blood on his shirt? Was he hurt?

She ran up to him as he approached the truck. "Sam, are you okay?"

He appeared puzzled. "Sure. Why wouldn't I be?"

She pointed to his shirt.

He grinned. "That's not my blood. Musta got that when I was dehorning." He turned and shouted to his men, "C'mon, boys, take a break."

"Be there in a minute," one of them called. Callie looked around Sam to the closest pen, where three of the men had a large calf immobilized in a tiny enclosure. She saw the flash of a knife, and before she could even guess at the wielder's intent, it happened. The calf made an unearthly screech.

"Oh, dear." She put a hand to her mouth and the other to her stomach to quell the sudden nausea.

"Callie?"

"What're they doing to the poor thing?" she asked.

"It's called castrating. Don't keep staring at it—for God's sake, you're white as paper."

EIGHT

Sam wrapped his hands around Callie's shoulders and forcibly turned her around so she couldn't see the gory scene that had mesmerized her. He marched her to the tailgate, moved a cooler full of lemonade, and sat her down. "You okay?"

She nodded weakly.

He grabbed a foil-wrapped packet of corn bread from a box and peeled it. "What are you doing here?"

"I wanted to see what y'all were up to."

"Well, you saw," he answered matter-of-factly.

"I thought I had a strong stomach, but apparently not."

"You get used to it. Here, want some corn bread?"

Her stomach roiled. "No, thanks."

Without comment he filled a plastic tumbler full of lemonade and handed it to her. That she could handle. She drank greedily.

"Ranching's not nearly as romantic as it sounds from a distance. But look."

"What?"

He pointed into a nearby pen. "There's the calf that was just castrated, branded, and dehorned."

Callie did look. The half-grown calf was milling about with its herd mates, grazing calmly. He seemed to have forgotten all about his recent ordeal.

"It seems so cruel," she murmured.

"It's not nice," Sam agreed, "but I guess I don't often think much about how the cattle feel. They're a commodity. They're my living."

She looked up at him. This was the part of Sam she didn't know, the part she'd never had the opportunity or perhaps taken the time to see.

Surprisingly, she found that this unfamiliar aspect of his personality was admirable, somehow, and gave him more depth. She could no longer think of him as the fun-loving boy she'd dated. He was a cowboy, and she admired the grit of any man who could do this for a living.

Especially this man.

She grinned foolishly, then reached into the box for a piece of corn bread. Her stomach was feeling better.

Sam got himself a bowl of chili, then sauntered back to lean against the truck near Callie. He cocked one skeptical eyebrow at her. "You still want to ride the roundup?" he asked smugly.

"Of course not. I can see now that I'd have just been in the way. But I would like to watch what you're doing here."

"Excuse me? You almost fainted a minute ago."

"That's because I wasn't prepared. I'm okay now. I

can handle it. This work is so much a part of you, Sam, and I want to understand it."

He grinned at the bit of flattery.

When the men were finished with lunch, Callie silently helped Rena pack up the leftovers and the trash. "I'm going to stay and watch."

Rena looked at her speculatively. "Why?"

"It's interesting." And she wasn't ready to leave Sam. She hadn't gotten her fill of seeing him flex his muscles beneath his Western shirt.

Rena shrugged. "It's your life." Without another word she climbed into the truck and drove off, leaving a wake of dust behind her.

Callie still wasn't thrilled by the sight of blood and the calves' pitiful bleating. When she'd had her fill, she wandered over to where the calves were penned, put her hand through the fence, and petted one of them on its scruffy neck. It shied away from her, snorting indignantly, and she laughed before finding a safer vantage point.

When the crew was done "processing" the calves, they loaded the steer calves onto huge transport trailers. They were being taken to a commercial feedlot, where they would spend the winter being fattened up for market. The females remained behind, to become part of the breeding herd.

The cows, newly separated from their babies, bellowed plaintively. Callie tried to harden her heart, like Sam, but she still felt sorry for the big animals.

She felt a nudge against the back of her leg. Turning swiftly, reflexes coiled, she was surprised to find a dog. He had definitely sought her out.

"Hey, I'm not one of your cows," she said indignantly to the German shepherd, who was hunkered down, panting, ears perked up, ready to play now that his day's work was done.

"Ah, I see you've met Punky."

Callie turned again at the sound of Sam's voice, and jumped when she realized he was leading a big brown horse behind him. She edged closer to the dog. "This is your prize cow dog?"

"He's a little more impressive when you see him at work. He did his job well today." Sam bent down to scratch the dog between the ears. "There's not a cow in my herd that ol' Punky can't get the best of."

Callie petted the dog cautiously. She'd always been a little bit afraid of big dogs, but not as scared as she was of horses. She kept the big brown one in her line of vision at all times, but it appeared exhausted and not intent on doing her any harm.

Her hand brushed against Sam's. Rather than pull away self-consciously, as she wanted to do, she let the touch linger.

Sam tipped back his disreputable hat and smiled like the devil. "So, what'd you think?"

"Dirty, messy work, like your mother warned me."

He looked decidedly disappointed. "We're still a ways from being done for the day. Have to dismantle these pens and get them ready for tomorrow. You can hitch a ride back to the house with the trailer."

Callie couldn't tell if Sam was giving her an option, or if she was being dismissed. Maybe he'd been testing her, and she should have shown more enthusiasm for his work.

"All right, I think I'd like to clean up before dinner."

"Would you tell Deana I love her, and I'll be home in time to tuck her in?"

"Sure." She turned toward the cattle trailer, but Sam stopped her with a hand to her shoulder.

"Callie."

"Yes?"

"Thanks for coming. It means a lot that you spent the day learning about my ranch, my work. I want you to like it here."

Callie didn't quite know how to respond. Why would he want her to like it here, unless he wanted her to *stay*?

Despite his promise, Sam didn't make it back to the house for dinner.

"He's just tending to a few details," Dalton said to Callie, eyeing her with unguarded speculation. All right, so she'd showered and washed her hair, changed into fresh clothes, and put on makeup. Was that such a big deal?

Callie wasn't the only one disappointed by Sam's absence. Deana was crying because she missed her daddy, and she wanted nothing to do with the tasty stew in front of her.

Callie sat down by Deana's high chair. She tried to remember how Millicent did it. Distract the kid, Callie decided. Focus on something other than food.

"Deana, you shoulda seen your daddy out there riding his horse," she began, not sure where she would go with this conversation. "He can make those cows go wherever he wants them to." Callie spooned up a bit of potato and broth and pretended to eat it. "Mmm, this is good. Anyway, your daddy and his horse—what's the horse's name?"

Deana showed a faint smile. "Clyde."

"Clyde, that's a good name," Callie said, delighted she was getting through. "Daddy and Clyde herded a whole bunch of cows onto this big truck. And they were all hollering—the cows, that is—'cause they'd been taken away from their mothers. And they were real sad."

Deana stared with rapt attention. Callie held a spoonful of diced roast beef up to the little girl's mouth. With her eyes still fixed on Callie, she opened her mouth and accepted the food.

Hey, this isn't so hard, Callie thought with a triumphant smile. "Where da cows go?" Deana asked.

"Well, they're being taken to a feedlot. Instead of having to eat grass, they'll be given oats and corn. They'll get such yummy food, and lots of it, so they'll forget all about their mamas and concentrate on growing up into great big cows. Er, steers, actually." And then they'll end up like this fella here in your bowl, she almost added, though she decided not to. Ranch baby or not, maybe Deana wasn't ready for the concept of where her meat actually came from.

Deana ate another bite of meat and some potatoes, and even a green bean. Before Callie knew it, the child had taken the spoon into her own hand and was shoveling stew mostly into her mouth.

When Sam finally made an appearance, Deana shrieked and nearly knocked the high chair over trying to get to him. With a sigh, Callie extracted her from the chair and set her down so she could run to her daddy.

"Deany!" Sam called out as he scooped his child into his arms. "Am I ever glad to see you. Did you miss me today?"

"Uh-huh," Deana answered, nodding vigorously. Then she launched into another of her monologues, which Callie simply couldn't understand, though Sam seemed to get the gist of it.

"I'll sit down and have some dinner in a minute," he said. "Right now, though, I need a shower in the worst way. Tell you what, later I'll split a piece of pie with you for dessert, how's that?"

Deana liked that idea.

Finally Sam focused on Callie. "Well."

'Bout time, she thought. She didn't gussy up for just anyone.

"Have you eaten?" he asked.

"I doubt she's had time," Beverly said. "She's been feeding Deana."

"Good." He gave Callie a searing look. "I'm glad you waited." With that he disappeared.

"I think Deana's eaten about all she's going to," Beverly said. "Why don't I get her ready for bed? I'll bring her back down in time for pie."

Callie appreciated Beverly's discretion, the subtle manner in which she'd cleared the way for Callie and Sam to eat alone so they could have some badly needed private time. She smiled her thanks.

After urging Deana on her way, Callie set the table in the formal dining room, since there would be only the two of them. On impulse she even lit a candle, then served up two bowls of stew, along with some leftover corn bread from this afternoon. She put it all in the oven to warm.

Unfortunately, her romantic candlelight dinner didn't turn out quite like she'd planned. Oh, Sam was appealing as ever, even in a sweatshirt and jeans, and he smelled so good Callie was tempted to climb right over the table toward him. But twice he nearly fell asleep with the fork halfway to his mouth. He was having a hard time following the conversation. She could see the weariness around his eyes.

"Sorry, darlin'." He shook his head. "Been a long day. But I bet if I had two minutes alone with you—I mean completely alone," he added, his eyes shining with a predatory gleam, "I'd perk up real quick."

Though they weren't about to be "completely alone," her heart beat faster at the thought.

The door opened, and Beverly cautiously peeked around the corner. "I was going to bring Deana down for pie, but she fell asleep on me."

Sam's expression was immediately contrite. "Damn. I worked so late today I didn't even get to spend time with my little girl."

"I'm sure she'll take a rain check," Beverly said diplomatically. "I forgot to tell you, Callie, that you had a phone call while you were out this afternoon."

"My mother?" she asked, hoping she'd gotten something interesting in the mail.

"No, it was a gentleman. He didn't leave a name, said he'd try back tomorrow."

Callie closed her eyes. Sloan. He was the only "gentleman" who knew where she was.

"Well, I'm turning in, kids," Beverly said, oblivious to the hard stare Sam was treating Callie to. "See you in the morning." She wore a cat-in-the-cream smile as she turned and left the room, apparently believing they were on the brink of some romantic interlude.

Romance appeared to be the last thing on Sam's mind at the moment. "What was that all about?"

She couldn't lie to him. "I'm sure it was Sloan Bennett. I asked him to call me."

"Why?"

"Because . . ." Well, heck, she might as well spit it out. "I had some thoughts about Johnny's death that I wanted to share with him. It's just possible that your father left a suicide note on his computer. He printed something out just before he died, but I don't think it's what he wanted to print out. He may have been distraught, confused, and he pushed the wrong buttons."

"Dammit, Callie, why do you have to keep after this? Can't we just put it behind us?"

She was bewildered by the fierceness of his attack. "Sam, a suicide note would put it to rest, don't you see?"

"It would already be to rest if you weren't meddling. I thought if I brought you out here—"

She threw her napkin onto the table and stood. "Is that what this is all about? Drag Callie to Nevada so she stays out of trouble?" Not so he could spend time with her. Not so she could learn about his work.

"That wasn't my original intention," he said, suddenly on the defensive. "I wanted you to come for me, for us too. I wouldn't have made love to you if I hadn't thought we had a second chance. But maybe that was just a pipe dream. Sometimes I think I don't know you at all, Callie."

Through a film of tears she looked down at the table, now a shambles of leftovers, dirty dishes, and melted candles. "I'll clean this up in the morning," she said. She couldn't bear to stay here, in this room, with Sam any longer.

She fled, and Sam made no attempt to stop her.

As she undressed, fighting back sobs, she acknowledged that coming to Roundrock was a bad idea. She'd told herself that she'd come for Beverly's sake, but perhaps she'd been harboring her own pipe dreams, no more substantial than wisps of smoke. She would have to go back home—immediately.

And then what? Maybe she would go on some job interviews, or work on some freelance story ideas. She could work on her Great American Novel, which she'd started several years ago and had three and a half pages done.

The prospects were downright depressing.

Callie slept in the next morning, deliberately missing Rena's breakfast and avoiding Sam. She realized, almost immediately, that she wouldn't make it home today. No one could be spared to drive her the four hours to Salt Lake City, where she could catch a plane.

So she devoted herself to mindless activity—checking phone messages, calling her mom, sending out résumés.

At close to noon she finally got hold of Sloan. "I think someone should go to the Sanger house and check out Johnny's computer," she told him. "Will is staying at the house. He's working nights, so he can let you in during the day." *If he's not trying to hide something.*

"Why the computer?"

Callie dutifully repeated the recent conversation she'd had with Beverly.

"Hmm. Printing up a week-old feed order would have been a very strange thing for Johnny to do just minutes before killing himself," Sloan concluded.

"Exactly. It had to be a mistake."

"You think he might have intended . . . oh. A suicide note."

"If you could find one, it might explain a lot of things."

"I'll get on it right away."

"Find someone who can sort files by date. Whatever he might have been doing that day would be the most recent file created. I don't think anyone has touched the computer since he died."

"Great. Thanks, Callie. Maybe we can wrap this thing up today."

"Yeah." She mumbled a closing pleasantry and hung up. She would like nothing better than to put all the questions behind them so she and Sam could get on with healing the rift between them her confounded reporter's instincts had caused.

Since the men were working closer to the house today, they returned for lunch. Rena served them huge helpings of ham and cheese for sandwiches, along with a hearty bean soup, lemonade, and coffee. Callie found herself playing hostess along with Rena, a role she didn't feel very comfortable with. It was hard to ignore Sam when she was serving him lunch.

"Sit down and eat, Callie," Sam said somewhat testily. "You don't need to wait on us hand and foot. We're big boys."

"You've been working hard." *And I haven't.* Again she was seized with that useless feeling, like she didn't belong.

"It's what we do best," Sam said. "Sit down."

She did, but she only nibbled on her sandwich, spending most of her time persuading Deana to eat and avoiding Sam's gaze.

Looking around, she noticed that the number of cowboys around the table seemed small. "Where's Mr. Cornelius?" she asked, recalling an older man who'd been there yesterday. "And the other guy, Travis?"

"They went up the road to help Lon Salem." Sam answered her question grudgingly. "He's the one who's got the pleuropneumonia outbreak. He stands to lose more than I do right now if he can't get it under control. I figured I could get by with a short crew today."

"That was before we knew how fast the weather was gonna come up on us," Dalton commented.

"Oh, is it getting cold?" Callie glanced out the window, surprised to see snow flurries.

"We'll get by." Sam stared down into his soup.

Callie wished there was something she could do, at the same time realizing she was completely helpless. Even if she could perform some useful function here, she doubted Sam wanted her help. Still, she felt compelled to offer.

"If there's anything I can do—"

"Just pray that we beat the snow," he said curtly. "I know waiting around isn't what *you* do best, but . . ." He shrugged, looking like he wanted to say more, but then he glanced around at the other men and apparently decided to hold his tongue. He turned his attention toward his daughter. "Deana? Doesn't look like you've eaten much of that soup."

"Too hot." She made a fanning motion with her hand.

"Try it again," Sam instructed patiently. She did, reluctantly sucking up a spoonful of the thick soup, managing to get more on her face than in her mouth. She made a face and dropped her spoon on the floor, daring anyone to reprimand her for it.

Sam rolled his eyes. "When roundup is over, young lady, we're going to work on mealtime manners."

"Oh, Sam, she's just a baby." Beverly wiped Deana's mouth with a napkin.

"Growing up too fast, if you ask me, and not learning a thing about how to be a lady." He added under his breath, "She's around too many rough cowboys."

"That could be remedied." Beverly gave Callie an oblique look.

Horrified, Callie pretended she didn't understand. She would have to have a talk with Beverly and tell her to *please* stop matchmaking.

There was only one other thing she had to do before Sam went back to work. "Will you walk outside with me?" she asked him.

He looked surprised by her request, but he didn't

deny her. "I have about five minutes before I need to get back."

She nodded. Unfortunately, it wouldn't take her even that long to let him know she would be leaving Roundrock as soon as she could catch a ride to Salt Lake.

She grabbed the first jacket she could find in the mudroom and rejoined Sam at the kitchen door. Wordlessly he held it open for her. A keen north wind met her as she stepped outside. The snow had stopped, but she had a feeling it would be back with a vengeance.

"Is there a problem?" Sam asked without preamble.

She halted midstride and turned to face him. "Yes. It's me . . . us. This isn't working out like either of us thought it would. I'm digging for the truth about your father's death—not for headlines, or public recognition, but because it needs to be done. I can't stop, just because you don't approve."

"Obviously not."

She noticed for the first time the raw, scraped knuckles on his right hand. She felt an incongruous urge to reach for him, to soothe the small hurt. Of course she didn't.

"I'm done trying to make you understand," she said. "I only wanted to let you know that I'll be leaving here at the first opportunity. I shouldn't have come."

She had succeeded in surprising him. His eyebrows shot up, and for an instant she thought she glimpsed a flash of pain in his eyes. But if she had seen it, it was quickly masked.

"Aren't you being a little hasty?" he asked.

"No. Sam, if you can't accept the fact that I can't sit

by and do nothing when I believe a crime has been committed, then we have nothing on which to base a relationship."

"Nothing? What about all those years we had together?"

"We were children."

"And what we shared the other day—"

"Was lust, pure and simple." She didn't really believe that. Their lovemaking had been special, transcending the mere satisfaction of physical desire. But they couldn't base a lasting relationship—and that *was* what they were talking about, talking around—on sexual compatibility alone.

Sam looked genuinely perplexed. "If you really want to leave, I won't stop you."

"Yes, I really do." It was too painful for her to stay, facing head-on the dream she'd denied herself, the dream she still couldn't have.

"It'll be a couple of days—"

"I know. Whenever you can spare someone to drive me to the airport. When you're done with roundup."

He nodded. "I'll drive you." He turned on his heel and walked swiftly toward his truck.

The real snow hit about three o'clock. Sam was out with Clyde and Punky, rounding up the last few stragglers, including a mean white-faced cow that was determined not to be rounded up.

"Git her, Punky," Sam called, watching with satisfaction as his dog nipped the old cow in the heels, showing her he wouldn't put up with any nonsense. She bellowed and tried to cut back toward the trees, but Sam headed her off.

Resigned, she eventually set off in the right direction, her calf following docilely behind.

Normally Sam assigned one of his men for this job, preferring to oversee the branding and whatnot. But today he'd craved solitude. He needed to think seriously about what his intentions were toward Callie, and whether he wanted to talk her into sticking around.

The question should have been easy. She wouldn't be happy here—not even for a couple of weeks—without hot stories to pursue and a new intrigue around every corner. He'd never had what it took to hold her, not eight years ago and not now. Nothing had really changed.

Then again, she hadn't even given Roundrock a chance. He'd practically forced her to bail out with the temper tantrum he'd thrown the night before.

Hell, maybe he'd overreacted to that phone call from Sloan Bennett. He'd been exhausted and had responded on pure instinct. But the whole idea of Callie dragging out his father's death really pushed a hot button. He hadn't handled the situation well at all. If only he could make Callie understand his position . . . *Or maybe if you tried to understand hers*, an inner voice whispered.

Sam pulled his hat down over his forehead to block the falling snow, then urged Clyde and the cow into a faster pace. He needed to get done here today and go back to the house. He needed to be with Callie. To what purpose, he didn't know. But he had to do something.

An hour later, cold and sore and bone-tired, he

made it back to the house. He didn't even bother stopping by his room to shower or change clothes. He went looking for Callie.

He found her in her room, sitting cross-legged on the bed, typing furiously on her laptop computer. "Oh, hi, Sam," she said in answer to his soft knock on her half-open door, sounding surprised to see him. The way she slapped the laptop closed made him wonder if she was writing something she didn't want him to see. "Are you finished working for the day?" she asked.

"Almost. I thought you might like to come down to the barn and see the horses. You said you wanted to see more of the ranch," he added.

By the expression on her face, she thought it an odd request. Sam wouldn't have been surprised if she'd turned him down flat. But she didn't.

"Oh, um, sure. Can I go dressed like this?" She was wearing a thigh-length sweater and leggings. "I don't have any boots."

"You'll do fine."

She cracked the computer open enough that she could shut it down, hopped off the bed, and put on her tennis shoes.

"What are you working on?"

His question made Callie decidedly nervous. "Oh, nothing important. I was just making some notes."

Callie's face was tight with tension as they walked together down the stairs. She was ominously silent as she donned her jacket and a pair of gloves he'd dug up for her. But the minute she stepped outside, her whole demeanor changed.

"Wow, it's snowing hard!" She zipped her jacket up

to the neck. "I didn't realize. Will it stick? Can we make a snowman later?"

Sam found himself smiling at Callie's delight. To him, snow was just a pain in the butt. But to her, it was a novelty. Destiny saw maybe half an inch of snow every five years or so.

She twirled around, as if trying to take it all in.

"The weatherman said it wouldn't stick," Sam said, "but who knows? The temperature's already close to freezing." The ground might be warm, but the white stuff was already clinging to trees, brush, and fences.

After a few moments, though, Callie's delight seemed to fade. She hugged herself against the brisk wind. "Sam, there's something I have to tell you. It's kind of important—pretty amazing, actually."

"I'm listening." And dreading.

"*The Washington Post* wants to interview me. I almost fainted when I listened to the message on my answering machine."

Whoa. Sam almost tripped over his own feet. "Did you call them back?"

"Uh-huh. We set up an interview for Monday. They'll fly me in. Think you can spare someone by then to drive me to Salt Lake?"

"This Monday?"

"Uh-huh. I never imagined they would consider some little upstart from Destiny, Texas. They'd start me out on features, but I could work my way up to a city beat."

"Sounds like they're really serious." Sam tried to smile. This was Callie's dream job, and she was closer than she'd ever been. But he felt a little dismal. Had he thought to catch her on the rebound from being fired and snag her into falling in love with his ranch? That was crazy. Just the same, he quietly resented the hell out of *The Washington Post* for calling her away.

"I think they really are serious," Callie said.

Sam wondered why she didn't say that with more enthusiasm.

NINE

They walked the rest of the way to the barn in silence. Callie's news had gone over like a bag of wet cement, and she didn't know quite what to say. She'd been dreaming of such a step up since her college days. Certainly she could understand Sam's lukewarm reaction, but why wasn't *she* more excited?

It was because of Sam. By all outward appearances, they didn't stand a chance as a couple. But there was always that small glimmer of hope—unless she took a job in Washington, D.C., worlds apart from Babcock, Nevada. That would lend a finality to their breakup that she wasn't yet ready to face.

For now, though, she pushed the matter out of her mind. Silly to agonize over it when the job was a long way from hers. Besides, she was curious about Roundrock's horses.

The barn was huge, much larger than it appeared from a distance, and it smelled not unpleasantly of hay and manure and a smell Callie vaguely identified as horseflesh. "There must be twenty stalls in here," she observed.

"Twenty-four. Back when Roundrock was over a hundred thousand acres and it had a bunkhouse full of cowboys, the stalls were filled. Now we have only eight horses, plus a couple of foals we might or might not keep."

She hesitated by the door. Sam literally had to pull her farther in. "The horses are locked in their stalls. They can't hurt you, even if they wanted to," he said, only slightly impatient.

She knew she was being silly. She was a grown woman, and she would have to get over her fear if she ever hoped to . . . Good Lord, hope to *what*? What dangerous ideas were bouncing around in her subconscious, anyway?

A month ago she hadn't given a flip about horses. Something odd was going on inside her.

Sam paused by a stall that housed a huge brown horse. "This is Stryker, our stud. He's no champion, and he's too mean to ride, but he produces decent quarter-horse stock. He's the only horse in this barn you need to be extra careful of." Just the same, Sam patted the stallion's nose.

One by one he introduced Callie to the rest of the herd, mostly mares and a few geldings. Nearly all of them were brown in color with black manes. She was frankly charmed by the foals, still kept with their mothers. One was different—a black filly with white stockings.

"I like this one." Callie bravely reached over the

stall door to pet the filly's velvety nose while its mother looked on suspiciously. "Will you keep her?"

"Mmm, doubtful. White stockings mean her hooves are weaker. She'd be better off as a pleasure mount. But she does have a nice disposition."

With one backward glance toward the sweet little horse, Callie followed Sam down the row of stalls. Dalton had his mount in the first stall, where he was rubbing the animal down with a foul-smelling liniment and cooing softly like the horse was a child.

"I have to rub down Clyde and see that he has enough bedding for the night," Sam said to Callie. "Want to help?"

She tried to squelch the panicky feeling that sprang up. He wanted her to actually go into a stall? "Um, I'd rather watch."

"Fine," he said, but Callie wasn't fooled by the feigned easiness of his answer. For whatever reason, he was anxious that she learn to like horses. And for whatever reason, she wanted to please him. A parting gesture, perhaps.

She would try. She promised herself that, at least. After all, the foal had won her over. No reason she couldn't convince herself to like big ol' Clyde too.

"After a hard day like today," Sam said, "this is what we rub 'em down with." He showed her a can, the same type of stuff Dalton was using, and a soft cotton rag. "But first we look for any cuts or saddle sores, and we treat it with this other stuff. Clyde, here, got a scratch on his foreleg when we were chasing down a real ornery cow and her calf today." Sam sprayed the small cut with something that turned it purple. "Keeps the flies off and helps prevent an infection."

Sam proceeded with the rubdown while Callie watched, fascinated—not because she had suddenly grown enamored of Clyde, but because the sight of Sam's strong hands moving with such sensitivity over the quivering horseflesh made her own flesh tremble. He did have magic in his hands. Even the horse could tell. With his eyes half-closed, and only the tip of his tail twitching, he was obviously enjoying his massage. He'd lost interest in the oats in his feeding trough.

Callie felt her own eyelids drooping as the sensual trance took hold. Then Dalton's strident voice broke the spell.

"You gonna fondle that horse all night or put him to bed?" the foreman asked, nudging his hat up with one forefinger. A corner of his mouth quirked up.

"He deserves a good rubdown." Sam's serious tone did not match Dalton's good-natured ribbing.

Dalton was quiet for a moment. "Well, unless you can think of something that needs doing, I'm heading up to the house for some supper. Seems to me I heard Rena say something about chicken and dumplings."

"Chicken?" Callie said with mock astonishment. "On a beef cattle ranch?"

"Hey, we have to watch our cholesterol like everyone else," Dalton said.

"I think we're done for the day." Sam capped the bottle of liniment. "I just want to put some more straw down, and we'll join you."

Dalton left with a tip of his hat, and suddenly the barn seemed a very quiet place. Callie became intensely aware of the isolation, made even more obvious by the cocoon of falling snow outside. "I'll help you with the straw," she piped up. The sooner they got the chores done, the sooner they could join the others at the house.

"Okay," Sam said. "In the fourth stall down you'll find a bunch of bails of straw and a pitchfork. Break off a chunk of straw with the pitchfork and bring it here."

"Um, okay." Callie had her doubts about her pitchfork-wielding abilities, but she was game to give it a try. She found the straw and the pitchfork. She even managed to skewer a chunk about the size of a spare tire and carry it precariously to Clyde's stall.

Sam looked up from fastening a blanket over the gelding's back. "That's it. Only I need about five times that much."

Callie sighed. "It'll take me five more trips, then."

"Hold on, I'll help. Just need to wash this stuff off my hands." He swung the stall door open and strode to a big utility sink at one end of the barn. He'd already removed his jacket. Now he unbuttoned his cuffs and rolled his sleeves up to the elbow.

Callie watched greedily. Why was it that, no matter how hopeless their relationship was, she never stopped wanting him?

When he was done, she followed him back to the straw supply. Callie simply stood out of the way as Sam used wire cutters to unfasten the bailing on the chunk she'd tried to dismember. He took the pitchfork from her when, just as he was about to show her how it was done, he paused, eyed the pile of straw, then turned and eyed Callie critically.

"What? Did I do something wrong?"

He flashed his best devilish smile, which went well with the pitchfork. "No, not at all." Suddenly his smile faded, replaced by a much more dangerous look. Hungry. Predatory.

She instinctively backed up, but found she had nowhere to go in the small confines of the stall.

He threw the pitchfork aside and took a step toward her as the implement hit the dirt with a thud.

"But—" She fell silent as she realized she wanted Sam, his body, his mind, his soul. She wanted to forget everything except the physical bond between them.

Sam reached behind him, snagging a horse blanket that was draped over the stall door. He tossed it onto the pile of hay, creating a makeshift bed in nothing flat.

She'd known there was something dangerous about this barn. But it had turned out not to be the horses.

Sam didn't touch her or close the distance between them. He was waiting for some sign of welcome, some sense that she wanted what he wanted. The call was hers.

Hell, there really was no choice to make. A little straw in her hair sure beat the pall that had fallen over them since their argument the night before. She didn't know whether Sam would ever understand her or approve of who she was. But she did know that their physical closeness meant something. It indicated understanding on some level. And maybe even forgiveness.

She reached for him.

The sudden heat between them took her breath away, literally. She'd known there was some pent-up desires waiting for an outlet, but she'd had no idea she and Sam would risk burning down the whole barn with their passion. But honest to God, it felt like flames surrounded them as they kissed, not only with lips and teeth and tongue, but putting their whole bodies into it. The cold temperature ceased to have any meaning.

Callie's body tingled in places she'd never imagined before. She grabbed Sam's wrists and guided his hands inside her jacket. They felt surprisingly warm, even through the thick cotton sweater she wore. Her breasts ached with longing as he teased the nipples to hardness with his thumbs.

His hat fell to the ground. Her jacket came off. He let go of her long enough to tug his boots off and pull at the laces of her tennis shoes. But then he was kissing her again.

"All those years," he murmured against her mouth. Then he seemed to deliberately halt whatever he'd been about to say.

She didn't press him. If he got all mushy on her, her choices would get a whole lot more complicated. She'd walked away from his love once; she wasn't sure she could do it again.

Perhaps he sensed that, because he said nothing more. He just kissed her and kissed her, never breaking contact even when he guided her toward the blanket-covered straw.

There was no playfulness this time as they tore their clothes off, the romance of disrobing each other giving way to the expediency of stripping down as quickly as possible. Callie hardly noticed the cold, especially when Sam pushed her down on the blanket and covered her with his big, hard body.

Still, despite his urgency, he didn't rush her. He

kissed her breasts until she was writhing with pleasure, sucking one nipple while he rolled the other between his thumb and forefinger with just the right amount of pressure. She tried to find some way of pleasuring him—stroking his chest, kneading his shoulders. But whether her caresses distracted him, or he simply didn't want her distracted, he put a stop to them by imprisoning both of her wrists in one strong hand, giving her a helpless feeling that was distinctly thrilling.

Maybe she enjoyed pretending she was his captive, she mused in a sensual haze, putting all the responsibility for their encounter on his shoulders.

"Please, Sam . . ."

"Please, what?" He'd shifted positions, so that now he was kissing her stomach, using his tongue to paint random patterns against her skin. She thought she was going to pass out from the novel sensations. And she'd thought that back when they were kids, they'd tried almost everything short of actual intercourse. Apparently they'd missed a few things.

"Please make love to me." Every word was an effort now. She was breathing hard, her breath kicking up steam in the cold barn. But she certainly wasn't cold.

He released her hands and moved up to lie beside her, slipping his arm behind her shoulders and pulling her against him. Their bodies touched from shoulders to toes in an incredibly intimate way. He simply held her, silent, the only sound their breathing and the occasional, distant snuffle of one of the horses. They were caught in a time warp on a sensual plane of their own making. Callie's urgency took a backseat to the sudden peace, the oneness she felt with Sam that was something close to sacred.

At last Sam nudged Callie onto her back again and found a place for himself in the cradle between her outstretched legs.

"Now, Sam," she urged him, feeling restless again, almost crazy with longing. She wondered how they'd waited this long, how she'd kept from cornering him and releasing their pent-up, long-denied passions.

He entered her with one quick, gliding thrust, filling her so completely, so perfectly, that she thought she might skip dying altogether and ascend straight to heaven.

But it only got better as Sam began to move, slowly at first, then faster, grasping her hips so that each penetration was as deep as possible.

Their coupling was necessarily short but oh so sweet. Once again Callie found herself in that place discovered only by lovers in perfect communion. She cried out her joy as tears filled her eyes. With a final series of quick thrusts Sam reached his peak, issuing the most primal, guttural sound she'd ever heard him make—so unlike her normally reserved Sam.

There might have been moisture in his eyes, too, though he surely would never admit to it. After one last cry, his body went from rigid to totally relaxed. He covered her like a blanket, blocking her from the cool autumn air.

Suddenly Callie had an attack of giggles. "Sam Sanger, I can't believe we just made love in a horse barn!"

He raised up on one elbow and smiled at her, but it

was a wistful smile. "This isn't really how I want it to be for us, Callie."

Though he was dog-tired after a day of repairing a windmill that would provide water for his cattle over the winter, Sam stayed awake, listening for the sound of his car. He'd let Callie borrow his Audi and drive herself to Salt Lake City to catch her plane to D.C. It had saved him a lot of driving, he reasoned, and he had other vehicles he could use. Besides, if she had his car, she would have to come back to Roundrock, if only to return the vehicle.

Ever since they'd made love in the barn she'd said nothing more about going home early, and he certainly hadn't brought the subject back up. He hoped she'd changed her mind. If they were ever to have a chance together . . . ah, hell, who was he kidding? They didn't have a chance, and never had. If she didn't get this job in Washington, she'd get another someplace else. He had nothing to offer her, nothing that could hold her for long, except his love.

That hadn't been enough eight years ago. It wouldn't be enough now.

So why was he sitting here, nervous as a calf about to be branded, waiting for Callie to get home? It was after eleven. What if something had happened to her? She had her cellular phone and his motor-club number, but he couldn't help worrying.

At eleven-twenty he finally heard the engine whine and the crunch of gravel under tires. With more energy than seemed possible, given the day he'd had, he leaped from the sofa and strode purposefully toward the kitchen door leading out to the garage.

Callie beat him to the door. She opened it just as he reached it. Her face was etched with the weariness of travel, and something else, some emotion he couldn't quite identify.

She skidded to a halt when she saw him. "You're still up. Worried about your car?"

"Worried about you. Those are some icy, lonely roads you were driving late at night."

"The roads were fine. I'm fine. But thanks for worrying." She didn't volunteer anything else.

Sam knew better than to grill Callie the moment she got in the door. He helped her off with her coat and poured her a cup of the decaf coffee he'd brewed.

"I have a message for you from Sloan Bennett."

That caught her attention. "What is it?"

"They found a suicide note on Dad's computer, just like you thought they would."

"Oh." She sank into one of the kitchen chairs. "I guess that settles things, then."

"Appears that way."

"You aren't going to say 'I told you so'?"

"Wasn't planning on it." He poured himself some coffee and sat down beside her. "I'm grateful to you, actually. If not for your digging around, that note never would have been found. And the note *does* finalize things. Now Mom won't have to worry about it anymore."

"Yes, that's good," Callie said absently. But she was staring off into space, stirring but not drinking her coffee.

"How was your flight?" Sam asked, easing his way into asking about the trip in general. Now that the matter of his father's death was settled, he and Callie had nothing left to fight about.

"Oh, fine. No problems. Both flights were right on time."

They were silent for a few moments. An old pendulum clock on the wall ticked with an exaggerated volume, causing Sam to wonder why he'd never noticed it before.

"So?" he finally said. "I'm dying here. How'd it go?"

The relaxed expression on her face vanished at once, replaced by wariness. "It went fine. The editor who interviewed me is very nice, and I think I made a favorable impression, although I told her about going to the city council meeting in stocking feet."

Sam smiled at that. Callie might be a little scattered sometimes, but that didn't undermine her competence. She was good at her job. Too damn good. He almost wished she wasn't. If she were only mediocre, it would be much easier for him to ask her to give it up.

"And how did she impress you?" Sam asked. "Is it a job you'd like to have?"

Callie took a deep breath. "It's the job I've dreamed about my whole life," she answered. "To be part of the Washington crowd, hobnobbing with politicians and lobbyists . . . A journalist in Washington can influence public policy. Even though I'd be a features writer at first, I'd be there. I'd be on my way."

Well, that pretty much answered that, Sam thought glumly. All that was left now was whether the *Post* offered the job to Callie. Maybe there were a lot of candidates, but he thought that any paper would be nuts to turn down Callie's experience, her judgment, her enthusiasm, which shone through every story she wrote.

"So do you think you'll get it? I mean, what are the chances?" Sam asked. At this point he wanted to leave no stone unturned. He wanted to know where he stood.

She shrugged uneasily. "Nothing's been decided yet."

And that, he thought, helped him not one iota. He rubbed her arm through her suit jacket, a jacket that, he realized, he'd never seen before. "You weren't wearing this when you left this morning."

"I bought the suit in Salt Lake and wore it out of the store. My old clothes are . . . oh, I guess I left them in the car. I'd better get them." She started to rise, but Sam held her in her chair.

"Forget the damn clothes." He leaned close to nuzzle her ear. "I want to take you upstairs and make love to you right now."

"Oh." Her eyes widened. "I'd . . . like that, too, but you know we—"

"Yeah, yeah, I know." He cut her off impatiently. "I've heard it before. We can't because it's not proper, because it would embarrass my mother, because Deana might wander in. We can't because we aren't married." And the fact that he couldn't lay claim to her made him suddenly furious.

"Everything you've said is true." She frowned, obviously sharing his frustration.

"Then let's fix it," he said suddenly. "If you don't

get that job, why don't you marry me and stay right here."

Callie's heart swelled and she couldn't seem to breathe in any air. Sam wanted to marry her? Oh, good gracious. She felt like she was going to faint.

"That didn't come out exactly the way I'd planned." Sam leaned forward, his eyes burning with an intensity the likes of which Callie had never seen. "Matter of fact, I hadn't planned it at all. But I realized today, while you were gone, that if I don't put my bid in, you'll be gone to another job halfway across the country, and I will have lost my chance."

"This is so sudden—"

"Not really. I wanted you to be my wife eight years ago, and I still do. Even when I was married, I used to imagine what it would be like if you'd have been the one to say yes, instead of Debra."

"Oh, Sam . . ."

"Now, don't answer right away," he said. "Think about it. It's not like you'd be stuck here with nothing to do. You could start your own newspaper, for instance. Be your own publisher."

"My own . . ."

"There used to be a pretty good little weekly out of Babcock, but old Mr. Kennafick died ten years ago and no one else has picked up the reins. The building and all the equipment are still there, and I bet we could pick it up for a song."

"Me? A publisher?"

"And if you don't like that idea, there's that novel you've always wanted to write."

"But I don't exactly fit in at the ranch, Sam."

"You'd learn. There are lots of things you can do if you have a hankering to be useful around here. Like helping to care for the horses and take hay to the cattle, if it snows. I bet you're a whiz with managing the books too. My office work needs some attention. . . ." His voice trailed off. "There are plenty of things you're qualified to do. That's the only point I'm trying to make. You can contribute as much to Roundrock as you like. Or as little, if some other activity takes your fancy."

An enthusiastic *Yes!* was bubbling at the back of Callie's throat, but she swallowed determinedly. She loved Sam—always had, no matter how hard she'd tried to forget him. And her deepest, darkest secret, the thing she'd never told anyone, was that sometimes she believed she'd screwed up royally by not marrying him in the first place. But she couldn't just change the whole course of her life with one impulsive word. She had to think about this.

Think? a sarcastic voice in her head mocked her. *What else have you been doing for the last couple of weeks?* In the back of her mind, she had been wondering how she could fit in here, and he'd told her. She wouldn't have to give up her career; she'd just give it a new twist.

Callie Sanger, Publisher. Nice ring.

Suddenly she felt like a kid in an ice-cream store. Too many flavors, too many choices. Except, oddly enough, this choice was much easier than it should have been. "Yes, I'll marry you, Sam."

He stared at her for what seemed like at least a minute, obviously not having expected such an easy victory. She felt semihysterical laughter rising like a tide, trying to escape.

"What's wrong, Sam? If you didn't want me to say yes, you shouldn't have asked."

"It's just . . . I thought you'd wait and see if they offered you the job first. I mean, you yourself said it was the opportunity of a lifetime—"

"I don't have to wait. I sacrificed marrying you for my career once already, and I know now that it was a mistake. Even though I haven't exactly fit in seamlessly here at Roundrock, I *want* to belong. I can do it, if I set my mind to it. I want to learn to ride and help take care of the horses, and I want to write my novel and bake pies and . . . and maybe publish a newspaper in Babcock. And if you wouldn't mind me doing a few freelance stories for bigger papers now and then, just so I don't get stale—"

"Of course I wouldn't mind. But, Callie, this is serious. I couldn't live with myself if you turned down the *Post* job for me. What if you got bored here? Then you'd blame me for tearing you away from your dream job—"

"I'm not Debra," she said quietly, but forcefully. "I'm responsible for my own life, my own decisions, thank you very much. I wouldn't blame you if I were incapable of creating a life here that would make me happy."

"Maybe not. Maybe you'd just up and leave."

A tense silence hung between them until Callie spoke again. "I can't believe you think that little of me." Or was it himself he thought little of? Because he'd lost Callie once, and then Debra had walked out on him? With his history, she shouldn't blame him for fearing the worst. But how could she convince him that she was no longer that immature, tunnel-visioned girl who'd said no to his proposal a lifetime ago? She'd seen a lot more of life. And she knew what she wanted—she'd figured that out in the fast-paced, anonymous city of Washington, D.C. She wanted Sam.

"You're right," Sam said. "That wasn't a fair statement. I know you wouldn't leave me, once you'd made the commitment. But I wouldn't want you to stay, if you were unhappy. I want you to be happy."

His words were so earnest, they brought moisture to her eyes. She swallowed back the tears. "I wouldn't be unhappy here. I'm sure of that. Just because I love being a journalist doesn't mean I can't love some other way of life. I've grown up. I've learned to be adaptable."

He smiled faintly. Then suddenly slapped his palms on the tabletop, startling Callie. "Okay, I have a compromise. If they offer you the job, you'll try it for a while. I'll be here, waiting for you, and the marriage proposal will stand. And after a year or so, if you still feel like you'd be happier on Roundrock, then we can get married and you'll never wonder if you made the right choice."

A year? Good Lord, no! "But, Sam, I know what the right choice is. I know it with my whole heart and soul."

But he was shaking his head. "It has to be this way, Callie. For my peace of mind."

Great, just great! What Sam didn't know was that she'd already been offered the job, right on the spot. The editor at the *Post* who'd interviewed her, Gloria Reames, had taken an instant liking to Callie. They'd quickly built a rapport, and before Callie knew what was happening, the job was hers if she wanted it.

Frankly terrified, she'd told Gloria she would have to think about it for a few days. But now the decision was surprisingly easy. She didn't want a job at the *Post*. She wanted Sam and Deana, and the other children she and Sam might have one day.

It was a cinch she couldn't tell Sam about the job offer now, or he'd shuffle her off to D.C. for the next year, whether she wanted to be there or not. "All right, Sam." She touched his beard-shadowed face. "I agree to your silly condition."

Now he smiled without reservation. "The time will go by quickly, you'll see." Then he was kissing her, and Callie lost herself in the feel of his mouth, his warm breath against her face, his soft hair sifting through her fingers. And she knew with every fiber of her being that they belonged together.

"And no more secrets between us, agreed?" Sam murmured, nibbling her ear. "I know we don't see eye to eye on everything, but we can always talk things out."

"Argue, you mean," Callie said with a chuckle. But immediately she sobered. There was already a secret between them. She should tell him that the D.C. job was hers for the asking, and then convince him not to make her delay their marriage because of it. But somehow, she couldn't find the courage to spoil the moment.

Tomorrow she would call Gloria Reames and tell her she'd decided not to take the job, and then put the whole thing behind her. Sam would never have to know.

"Sure you can hack it, married to a cowboy?" Sam asked, holding her close.

He'd meant the question in jest, but Callie felt a little shiver run down her spine. She'd always claimed she didn't believe in fate or psychic predictions from gypsies or newspaper horoscopes, but here she was falling headlong into marriage with a cowboy—the one thing she'd sworn she wouldn't do. And the one thing Theodora had claimed, with uncanny certainty, that she would do.

TEN

As Callie sat in her favorite frozen-yogurt shop in Destiny, waiting for Sloan Bennett to show up, she mentally went over her list of things to do. One of those things was to call up Gloria Reames and tell her she couldn't take the job. She'd been procrastinating for days.

But now she wondered: Was she hedging her bets in case her marriage plans with Sam fell through? She wouldn't change her mind, but what if he did? Surely not. Surely she had more faith in him. The wedding was in less than two weeks. Once a decision had been made, plans had accelerated at the speed of light. Even though she was feeling a little shell-shocked by the whole thing, he hadn't once expressed any doubt.

Her delay in calling Gloria was simply avoidance of something unpleasant, she told herself. Besides, she was working furiously on her idea for the Greenhorn at the Ranch story—which might possibly become a Greenhorn Marries Rancher story—and she wanted to have the details nailed down before she talked to the editor.

This meeting with Sloan was another unpleasant necessity. There were loose ends to tie up. She wanted her part in the Sanger investigation to be a closed book before she saw Sam again.

"So, how's the blushing bride today?" said Sloan's voice from behind her. She jumped, and he laughed. She'd been so lost in her thoughts that she hadn't even seen him come in. He set a chocolate milkshake in front of her, then found a chair. "The milkshakes are on me—call it gratitude for helping us close the book on the Sanger investigation for good."

Callie said nothing. There was something nibbling at her subconscious, something uncomfortable.

"Callie, what's wrong?" Sloan leaned forward, peering at her face.

"It's just that—and I can't believe I'm saying this—but something still doesn't feel right."

Sloan frowned. "Like what?"

"Like, the note wasn't written in Johnny's own hand, so how do we know he really wrote it? And why wouldn't he handwrite it and sign it properly? And why didn't he notice that he'd printed out the feed order instead of the note, and correct the matter?" Callie hadn't even realized she'd been harboring these doubts in the back of her mind until now. Like everyone else, she'd wanted to—tried to—put the tragic matter out of her mind.

She especially hated bringing any doubts to light now, because her so-called meddling was bound to be a point of contention between her and Sam.

"So your theory is that someone killed Johnny, tapped the note out on his computer while he was still bleeding, tried to print it out, but in haste printed the wrong thing—"

"Maybe the murderer wasn't familiar with the computer."

Sloan seemed to be thinking. After a long minute he shook his head. "Sorry, Callie. I can't buy into this one. I think Johnny simply wrote his note on the computer because it was easiest. It's cumbersome to handwrite things after you get spoiled by word processing."

Sloan had a point. All right. So this time she'd let it drop. She'd done her part, she'd voiced her doubts.

"Okay," she said with a nod. "I'm done playing Nancy Drew. I have a wedding to plan. Which brings me to the other reason I asked to meet with you. I want to hire an off-duty police officer to help with parking at the church. Would you be interested?"

Sloan smiled. "Sure. As long as I can come inside the church after the traffic dies down and watch you and ol' Sam getting hitched. About time."

If we ever do get hitched, Callie thought an hour later as she stood on the Sangers' front porch, feeling over the door frame for the key she knew was there. She still didn't have a dress. Beverly had graciously offered her own wedding dress of thirty-five years ago, lovingly preserved and stored in her closet. "You know where the key is," Beverly had told her. "Just go on over there anytime and try it on. And while you're there, could you water the houseplants? I'm sure Will won't remember."

Callie's hand closed over the key. She let herself into the stuffy house. Since it was relatively warm outside for a November day, she left the door open to allow some fresh air in. Then she went to Beverly's bedroom. Feeling a bit like a voyeur, she pawed around in the closet until she found what she was looking for, on a high shelf in the very back.

She brought the box out into the light and sucked in a breath of pure delight. The plain satin dress, the color aged to a delicious ecru, was like something a princess would wear. The veil, attached to a circlet of pearls, added to the image. Callie took it out of its protective housing, shook it out, and tried it on.

It fit perfectly.

"Hah, one problem solved," she said aloud as she gingerly stepped out of the dress. She folded it gently and returned it to the box. Now she would have to go to the mall to find some ecru satin pumps, and she would be set.

Callie finished up by watering the plants, which were indeed looking a bit droopy. She returned the watering can to the back porch and gave one final look around before heading out. That's when she noticed the office door ajar.

Had the cleaning service come? she wondered. Had they done a good job? She couldn't resist taking a quick peek.

The office was practically sterile in its cleanliness. No unpleasant odor lingered, just the aroma of furniture polish and glass cleaner. The desk chair was gone, she noticed—probably unsalvageable. She was about to withdraw when an overwhelming temptation overtook her.

Johnny's computer. The suicide note. Would the police have left it on the hard drive, or erased it?

In moments the machine was humming. It was identical to the one she had at home, so she had no trouble cranking up the file management program. All she had to do was ask for word-processing files by date, starting with the most recent.

And there it was, a file titled simply "note." She opened it, took a deep breath, and started reading:

> My Dearest Family,
> I don't see how I can go on. I'm exhausted from the constant struggle. Once I'm gone, you'll never have to worry again. I love you all. Please forgive me and remember me fondly.
> Yours, now God's,
> Johnny Sanger

The first thing that struck her was that the language wasn't Johnny's. He'd been a plain man of plain words. *My Dearest Family* and *remember me fondly* sounded like phrases out of a Victorian diary. But even as she was contemplating whether Sloan would entertain her suspicions, she noticed something else. Upon closing the file, she was back in file management, where the date of the note's creation was clearly listed.

A date that was two days after Johnny's death.

It took a few seconds for the full implication to hit her. Johnny hadn't written this note. A murderer had. Good heavens, how could the police be so incompetent? Whoever Sloan had brought over to log onto Johnny's computer obviously hadn't known what to look for. Once again, they'd been anxious to grab onto any clue—even a cleverly manufactured one—in order to close the case quickly.

Callie heard a car engine coming up the driveway. Her hands shaking, she quickly closed the file, then shut down the computer. It wouldn't do for anyone to catch her in here. She had to get away, then she had to contact Sloan. There was no doubt in her mind that Johnny had been murdered, and the murderer had taken the opportunity to create some handy evidence once all eyes were off the death scene.

But who? Any number of people had been at the house after the death, to pay their respects. And the family had all been here, of course.

She hightailed it out of Johnny's office just as the front door opened. Wheeling around the corner, she came face-to-face with Will Sanger.

"Oh, you startled me," she said breathlessly. Another ten seconds, and he'd have seen her coming out of that office.

"Same here. What are you—"

She held up Beverly's wedding dress as evidence of her innocent intentions. "Your mom said I could try on her wedding dress. It fits, so I'm borrowing it."

"Oh. Uh-huh." He looked uncomfortable, tunneling his fingers through his short brown hair. Would he be able to tell she'd been snooping? Had she left some trail behind her? She wasn't a computer expert by any means.

"Well, guess I'll be going. I watered the plants."

"Oh. Good. Mom asked me to, but I forgot, what with all the other stuff there is to do around here."

Like manufacturing evidence? "Um, I'll just be on my way."

"Okay. By the way, congratulations to you and Sam."

"Thanks." She couldn't get out of there fast enough.

As soon as she was a good mile away from the Sanger place, she pulled over and used her cellular phone to call Sloan. Amazingly, she caught him in his squad car.

"I just pulled up to the mall to handle a shoplifting incident, and I'm kind of in a hurry," Sloan said.

"It's important."

"All right, all right. Meet me in the food court at the mall in twenty minutes. I'm almost off duty anyway."

"But, Sloan—" It was too late. He'd disconnected.

She didn't really want to go to the mall right now. Sam and Deana were driving in from D/FW Airport, due in a half hour or so, and she'd told Sam she would be home when they arrived. But she supposed her absence couldn't be helped. She had proof—*proof*—that Johnny had been murdered. This wasn't something she could sweep under the rug.

And Will had seen her at the house. She might actually be in danger.

She made it to the mall with ten minutes to spare. Which store had Sloan been called to? she wondered. She walked from one end of the mall to the other but didn't see him. Now she wished she hadn't left her cellular in the car. If Sloan was detained, he might try to call her and let her know not to wait for him.

By the time she reached the food court, it had been almost twenty minutes. She sat down to wait, something she wasn't very good at. She fidgeted, feeling definitely paranoid.

That's when she saw Tamra, walking briskly toward the food court as if she were on some important mission. Callie started to wave and call out to her future sister-in-law, then abruptly shrank back when she saw the table toward which Tamra was headed.

Nicole Johnson was already sitting there, waiting.

Now, what kind of business did those two have?

Intrigued, Callie moved to a table that was mostly concealed from the rest of the food court by a potted tree, then peered between the leaves at the two women. Neither of them had bought anything to eat or drink, which made Callie suspect this wasn't exactly a social meeting.

Callie couldn't stand it. She was dying to know what those two women were talking about. You can take the girl out of the newspaper, but you can't take the newspaper out of the girl, she caught herself thinking.

Before long, it became apparent that Tamra and Nicole were arguing. Although Callie couldn't understand the words, she could hear the shrill tones drifting across to her every so often. And Nicole's body language, especially, was telling. She was leaning forward aggressively, her attractive face spoiled with an ugly scowl. From time to time she shook a finger at Tamra.

After about five minutes of this Nicole stood up, shoved her purse strap over her shoulder, and flounced away.

Tamra sat very still, her head in her hands, the picture of dejection. But slowly her head came up. She stared after Nicole's retreating form, as if mesmerized. Then, suddenly, she stood up herself, and with a sense of purpose etched into every line of her small, dainty face, she followed.

And Callie was right behind, her heart beating like a drum from a Sousa march. She had a feeling something important was going on here. She wanted to wait for Sloan, but if she did, she would lose her quarry. From a safe distance she followed, praying that both women were focused enough on their own problems that they wouldn't notice her.

Nicole went to her car, an older but well-maintained Cadillac—red, of course. Tamra lost herself in a crowd of teenagers, looking around furtively, ducking behind vans and lampposts like a third-rate secret agent.

Geez, Callie thought, why didn't the woman simply announce her presence with a bullhorn?

Callie kept the other two cars in sight as she unlocked her door, grateful they'd all three parked in the same lot. She started the engine, screeched out of her parking place, and stomped on the gas.

Tamra had turned right onto Revere Parkway, but now her beige Escort was out of sight. Callie chanced a look at her watch. Shoot, Sam was due to arrive any minute at her house.

Well, he'd just have to wait a bit.

She caught sight of Tamra's Escort again, stuck at a light. There was the red Cadillac too. Good. Callie pulled the cellular phone out of its case, lifted the handset, and dialed her home number. She got her answering machine.

"Sam? Sam, if you're there, please pick up." He didn't, so she continued. "I've been, um, unavoidably detained. Please just make yourself at home, raid the refrigerator, and I'll get there when I can." Impulsively she added, "I love you, Sam." The words, still so new and fresh, gave her a thrill.

She hung up, feeling guilty for making him wait. But if Tamra or Nicole was somehow involved in his father's murder, he would want someone to find out about it. He'd once said so, anyway.

Next she dialed the number of Sloan's cellular, but got no answer there. So she dialed the police station. She'd memorized both numbers during the last few weeks.

"I think Officer Bennett's off duty now," the operator said. "Did you try his cellular number?"

"No luck. How about Danny Fowler?" Callie asked.

"I'm sorry, he's off today."

Damn. "Okay, thanks." She disconnected, then dialed one last number—Sloan's answering machine at home. If he headed there after getting off duty, he might pick up the message.

"Hello, Sloan? It's Callie. Sorry I missed you at the mall. I saw Tamra Sanger and Nicole Johnson arguing. Now Tamra is following Nicole and I'm following Tamra. Please, if you get this, call me on my cellular." She gave him the number, her approximate location, and the direction she was headed. "Oh, and Sloan? I have proof that Johnny Sanger was murdered." There. If that didn't prompt him to call her back in a hurry, nothing would.

◆━━━━━◆

Sam pulled into the driveway and all the way back to Callie's carriage house. This last week without her had been pure hell, and he felt like a kid about to ride the roller coaster at the thought of seeing her again—excited, happy, and a little scared.

Their engagement had come so suddenly, so unexpectedly, that it almost didn't seem real. They'd had only a few days to come to terms with it before Callie was boarding a plane for home so she could plan the wedding. They'd spoken several times on the phone, and Callie had sounded excited and not the slightest bit unsure about their upcoming marriage. Still, he wouldn't lose the slightly queasy feeling in his stomach until he laid eyes on her again and knew for sure that all of their plans were still on.

She'd told him she was out of the running for the job at *The Washington Post.* He wasn't sure whether he was grateful about that or not. More than anything he'd wanted Callie to be sure of her decision to marry him and live on Roundrock, and if she still wanted to after a stint in D.C., then he would feel pretty confident that she knew what she was doing.

Then again, he didn't want to wait six months or a year for her. He wanted her back at the ranch with him and Deana. He wanted to start living the rest of their lives. He wanted to devote himself to making her happy. So from a purely selfish perspective, he was overjoyed at her continued unemployment.

"Daddy, I haffa go potty," Deana said.

"Soon as we get inside." Leaving his luggage for

later, he went to the front door and rang. It didn't surprise him when Callie didn't answer. She was always late. He found the extra key she left under a pot of geraniums, unlocked the door, and carried Deana up the stairs.

On the way to the bathroom with Deana, he noticed Callie's answering-machine light blinking. It occurred to him that the message might be for him. If she was running late, she would call to let him know. But he nixed the idea of listening to the message. Though he and Callie were soon to be husband and wife, she still had her privacy.

With potty chores taken care of, Sam went into the kitchen to see if he might find something to drink. The phone rang, and he resisted answering it. Let the machine get it, he thought. If it was for him, he'd know soon enough.

He heard Callie's voice on the outgoing message, and smiled. Even that tiny, impersonal bit of his fiancée warmed his heart.

"Hello, Callie, this is Gloria Reames from *The Washington Post*," the caller said into the machine.

Sam froze.

"I hadn't heard from you. Forgive me for being too anxious, but we hit it off so well when you interviewed that I'm really excited about the prospect of working with you. I hope you'll decide to come on board. Please call me at your earliest convenience." She recited the number. "Oh, and I received the fax you sent regarding the Greenhorn at the Ranch story, and I think it's fantastic. I'm looking forward to talking with you more about it."

The call disconnected—and so did Sam's heart. What in holy hell was going on? Callie'd been offered the reporter's job at the *Post*, that much was obvious. And she hadn't told him.

And what was this thing about a greenhorn at the ranch? It sounded as if Callie was using her experiences on Roundrock as the basis for a feature story, something to lure the *Post* into hiring her, perhaps.

Sam felt like he'd entered the Twilight Zone, where nothing was as it seemed. If Callie planned all along to continue her career, why hadn't she told him up front? Why all this nonsense about a wedding that would never take place? How had they gotten their wires so hopelessly crossed?

Privacy be damned. He wanted to listen to the message again. He pushed the appropriate button on the answering machine. It rewound for a long time, and when the messages began playing—including the calls that had come in before Sam's arrival—all he could do was stare in openmouthed shock.

"This is Mel Weston from the *Dallas Morning News*. I received your résumé, and I'd be interested in . . ."

"This is Allison Henson from the *Detroit Free Press*. I'd like to talk to you about a reporter's position we have coming open. . . ."

"Hi, Ms. Calloway, this is Leona Black from the *Miami Herald*. . . ."

Sam felt like he'd been kicked in the gut by a mule. Good God Almighty. Callie was a hot item. Her career was about to soar. No telling how far she could go.

And he absolutely couldn't marry her now.

If he took all these possibilities away from her, she

would never know what could have been. And she might very well grow to hate him for forcing her to give up the work she was obviously meant to do.

Then came a message from Callie herself, to him. "Unavoidably detained." He didn't even want to think about what she might be up to, but obviously lots of things had priority over him and Deana. The *I love you* at the end of the message was not at all comforting. If she truly loved him, how could she keep all these secrets from him?

Nicole's Cadillac pulled into a neat residential area. Although the houses were older, they were well maintained. Large shade trees on every lot gave the neighborhood a lazy, small-town feel. Callie didn't turn onto the same street. She pulled past, then slowed to see what Nicole and Tamra would do.

The Caddy pulled right into a driveway in the middle of the block. Tamra's Escort, some distance behind, slowed, then drove past Nicole's driveway and turned right at the corner.

Callie didn't believe for a minute that Tamra would now drive away, not after such a determined pursuit. Following her instincts, Callie drove to the next street parallel to Nicole's, turned right, and came out on the same street Tamra had turned on, though she was a block away.

Sure enough, Tamra had stopped around the corner. The engine was running. Nothing was happening. Callie imagined that Tamra was weighing her options.

Callie's cellular phone beeped, making her jump.

She was a bundle of pure nerves. It took her a moment to realize the sound was a "low battery" indication. Damn. She hoped she could get one more call off. She tried to remember Sloan's cellular number, which she'd just dialed a few minutes ago, but suddenly her brain was paralyzed. So she called and left a message on her own answering machine, just in case.

"Sam? If you're there, please pick up. I'm on a cellular phone that's about to go dead, so I don't have time to explain, but if Sloan Bennett happens to call there, I'm at the corner of Woodland and Douglas. I think maybe Sloan should meet me here. I have a feeling we might have an ugly confrontation. Bye, Sam. I love you." She said it again, still reveling in the words and the meaning behind them.

She'd no sooner hung up than the phone rang. "Hello? Hello?"

"Callie? It's Sloan. What the hell is going on?"

"Oh, Sloan, I'm so glad you called. Tamra is following Nicole, sneaking around like she was up to no good." As she explained things to Sloan she kept her eye on Tamra's car. The driver's door opened, and Tamra climbed out.

"Listen, Callie," Sloan said, "you be careful. I'll meet you as soon as I can. Don't try to get any closer or confront either of those women, you understand?"

"I won't."

"Where are you?"

"I'm at—" That's when she spotted the shiny object in Tamra's hand. "Oh, Jesus, Sloan, she's got a gun!"

"Who?"

"Tamra! Oh, Sloan, come quick, I'm scared."

"Where are you?"

"I'm at Douglas and Woodland. . . ." Callie realized the phone was no longer working. Her battery had gone dead.

ELEVEN

Sam paced Callie's living room like a pent-up wild animal when the phone rang. He expected it to be another of the newspaper editors determined to hire Callie, so he didn't move to answer it. But when he realized it was Callie's voice coming over the answering machine, he lunged for the phone, intending to get some answers from her. But he wasn't fast enough.

He rewound the tape and listened to the message. What? Sloan Bennett again? Her ongoing association with this character was more than getting on his nerves. The jealousy rose up in him like an angry red tide.

When he listened to the message again, he noticed something else. Callie sounded worried. No, scared. And Sloan was a cop.

Dammit, if Callie was in trouble, why didn't she dial 911 like everyone else?

Sam quickly tamped down his frustration with Callie as another, more primitive emotion took over. Someone or something was threatening the woman he loved, and he was by God going to protect her. Douglas and Woodland, she'd said? He'd find the intersection, and he'd find her. He started for the door, then paused.

Deana. What could he do with Deana? He wasn't about to take his baby girl into a dangerous situation. The solution came with a knock on the front door. Sam ran down the stairs and opened it. Millicent Jones stood on the porch.

"Hi, Sam, I came over to see if I could help Callie with her—"

"I don't have time to explain," he said, cutting her off. He could apologize for his rudeness later. "Can you watch Deana for a few minutes? An emergency's come up."

"Well, of course, but—"

"Thanks a million, Millicent. I'll make it up to you." With that, he flew out the door, not even telling Deana good-bye.

Callie dropped the useless phone onto the passenger seat. Now what was she going to do? Tamra swiveled her head toward Callie's car, and Callie ducked down. Had Tamra seen her? Please, don't let her see me, she prayed.

After a few moments she risked a peek over the dashboard. Tamra was no longer carrying the gun in plain sight. She was walking determinedly down the sidewalk toward Nicole's house.

Callie had to stop her. She jumped out of the Nissan, careful to stay hidden behind the car. But Tamra didn't even look in Callie's direction. She was too full of purpose.

Callie sprinted to the house on the nearest corner, breathing a sigh of relief when she reached the front porch without being seen. A large forsythia bush shielded her from Tamra's view. She rang the doorbell and, when she didn't get an immediate response, pushed the button several times.

No one answered.

Tamra had reached Nicole's front door. Callie ran to the next house. No one answered the doorbell there, either. When a middle-aged woman answered her knock at the third house, Callie did all but drop to her knees and kiss the woman's feet.

"Hello, ma'am, could you please dial nine-one-one?" she asked in her calmest voice. She didn't want the woman to think she was a wacko. "There's an emergency taking place at that house right there."

The woman squinted in the direction Callie pointed. "Which house?"

"The yellow one. I think Nicole Johnson lives there."

"Oh, well, there's no telling what kind of trouble she's up to. What kind of emergency?" the woman asked dubiously.

"Someone with a gun," Callie said. "Please, hurry."

The woman's eyes grew large. "An angry wife, no doubt. No more'n she deserves. But I'll call the cops if you want."

"Please. And tell them to hurry!"

That taken care of, Callie considered her options. Tamra had entered Nicole's house. At least, she wasn't on the porch anymore. Either Nicole had let her in, or she'd forced her way. Callie figured that whatever was happening behind those four walls, neither woman would be looking out the window. She decided to risk moving closer.

She zipped from bush to tree to parked car like some half-baked spy, all the while knowing any idiot with half an eye would spot her. She was just hoping that if bullets started to fly, she would have something to duck behind.

But so far all was quiet. It was only when she came right up to Nicole's yellow frame house, flattening herself against the wall, that she could hear the angry voices through a window that had a BB hole in it.

"You got some nerve," Nicole was saying in her nasal Texas accent, "trying to bleed more money out of me after what's happened. I only let you get away with it before because I didn't want Johnny humiliated. But he's dead, now. I don't care. So you just go ahead and tell the world I was sleeping with Johnny, even though I wasn't. And I'll tell the world your husband killed him."

Oh, Lord, Callie was thinking, hardly daring to breathe. Don't threaten her, Nicole. Didn't she realize Tamra was dangerous?

A charged silence followed Nicole's declaration. "Murder? What are you talking about?" Tamra asked, sounding not in the least convincing in her bewilderment. "Johnny committed suicide—probably over his guilt for getting involved with you."

"Hah! Not likely. I knew from the very beginning that Johnny hadn't killed hisself. I even went and talked to Callie Calloway about it, when she was still at the paper."

Callie cringed upon hearing her name.

"Johnny was happier than he'd been in a long time," Nicole continued. "So I knew something was up. But it wasn't until I saw the crime-scene photos that I figured out what it was."

"How could you possibly—"

"Havin' a daddy who's a police chief comes in handy, sometimes. I asked him to let me see the pictures, even though it liked to kill me seeing Johnny all laid out like that. It didn't take me long to figure out what was wrong—aside from the fact that his office was torn to pieces and he'd never leave this world with a mess like that behind him."

"So what did you 'figure out'?" Tamra asked with false bravado. "What did you see that the police and Callie and everyone else missed?"

"It was real simple. His right hand was wrapped around the shotgun's trigger. But he was left-handed."

Callie closed her eyes. Of course. Damn, it *was* simple. How could she have missed it? The police might not have known to question whether he was left- or right-handed, but Callie had known he was a lefty. That's what had seemed out of kilter, but she hadn't been able to put her finger on it.

"That doesn't mean anything," Tamra said.

"To the police, it would. I've learned a few things about murder investigations, being the chief's daughter and all. And when the police figure out it was a murder, guess who their prime suspect will be? Who was at the house, alone with him? Who's going to benefit from that insurance money? And who's got a criminal record, hmm?"

"Will didn't kill his stepfather," Tamra said flatly.

"Maybe not. But if you say one word to anyone about my friendship with Johnny, I'll have a talk with my father about Johnny being a lefty, and I might let it slip that you was blackmailing me. And we'll see where the chips fall. Now, you get outta here before I call the cops and report you trespassing."

A long silence followed. Callie prayed some more. Please, Tamra, do what she says.

Finally Tamra spoke. "I don't think so."

Callie could hear Nicole's heels clicking across a hardwood floor. "You don't think I'd do it?"

"Don't touch the phone." Tamra's voice was low, almost a growl, and it gave Callie chills.

"Tamra? For God's sake, honey, put that thing away. What are you doing?" Nicole's voice shook.

Callie whispered a curse. Tamra had obviously taken out her gun. Callie was itching to peer through the window, but she didn't dare. Still, if Tamra really intended to shoot the thing, Callie had to do something to prevent it. She couldn't stand by and let Tamra commit cold-blooded murder.

Why didn't the police come?

"I'm protecting what's mine," Tamra said in answer to Nicole's question. "I worked too hard for this. Do you have any idea how long I've been waiting for the payoff?"

"Good God, you're admitting that Will murdered Johnny?"

Tamra laughed without humor. "Will? He was always such a talker, claiming how he was going to be an important, wealthy man someday. And I fell for it. You shoulda seen those letters he wrote to me from prison. But when it came right down to seizing an opportunity, he was a big fat zero. He wouldn't have anything to do with blackmail—too afraid of going back to prison. I had to take matters into my own hands."

"Don't tell me you killed Johnny," Nicole said, challenging.

"You bet, and a damn good job I did of it, too, making it look like suicide. After the first shot stunned him, I wrapped his hand around the gun for the second shot so there'd be powder residue on his hand. Wrong hand, though," Tamra muttered.

"But . . ." Nicole faltered. "He was alive when you and Beverly went to the store. . . ."

"Huh-uh. *I* started up the printer so Beverly would hear it and think Johnny was working."

Callie slowly released her pent-up breath. Everything was exactly as she'd theorized—except she'd pictured Will as the murderer, not timid little Tamra.

"But the note—" Nicole objected.

"The note was something I dreamed up later, to hedge my bets. That worked out well, too, don't you think?"

"I don't believe you," Nicole said flatly. "How could a little thing like you possibly overpower Johnny?"

"A big ol' shotgun is a powerful equalizer," Tamra bragged. "I waited until he was drinking, then I went into his office and threatened to tell Beverly about his affair with you if he didn't pay me off. Then he told me about the insurance. He tore that office apart until he found the policy to show me. Said if I'd be patient, I'd have a lot of money in a year or so. Said he had cancer. But I was tired of waiting. Like I said, I know when to seize an opportunity. Good thing, too, since he was lying about being sick."

"Why, you despicable little tramp! Go ahead, shoot me if you want to. The police will catch you, and easy too. Someone will see you leaving the house. Someone will see your car. Someone might have seen us talking at the mall."

"If I make it look like another suicide, all that won't matter. Tell me, Nicole, are you right- or left-handed? I don't want to make the same mistake twice."

Callie had to do something. She had to stall Tamra with a diversion of some sort. A rake was leaning up against the side of the house near the back porch. Impulsively, Callie seized it, ran back to the living-room window, and bashed the handle through the glass. Then she ran for the back of the house.

Breathing hard, she stood by the back door, giving Tamra a few seconds to investigate the broken window. Then Callie used the rake to break the glass in the back door. She took off running again, around to the far side of the house, keeping close to the outside wall, ducking when she crossed in front of windows.

She counted to thirty, broke another window, and set off again in a low, crouched run. She didn't count on coming around the corner and running directly into Sam.

They both nearly fell to the ground from the force of the impact. "Sam? Down, get down," she hissed, dragging him into a crouch with her.

"Have you lost your mind?"

"I know this looks bad, Sam, but Tamra's in there with Nicole Johnson, and she has a gun. I think she was about to kill her, and I was creating a diversion by breaking windows. The police are on their way." Supposedly. If that neighbor had called 911 like she promised.

"Tamra? My sister-in-law? With a gun? Are you sure?"

"Shh! Lower your voice. I'll explain it all later." She looked around, assessing their situation. "I think maybe we should stay put now. This overgrown bush hides us pretty well."

She heard the front door open. "Hey, who's out there?" Tamra called. "You better show yourself. I have a gun and I know how to use it."

Sam's face registered blatant shock.

"I told you," Callie whispered. "She killed your father."

Sam said nothing.

Suddenly a voice, low and deadly, spoke to them through the screen of greenery that shielded them. "Come out of there right now."

Callie held her breath.

"Oh, for God's sake," Sam said. He parted the bushes, walked straight up to Tamra, and grabbed the gun out of her hand before she had time to even react.

She stared, uncomprehending, at her empty hand.

"What the hell did you think you were doing?" Sam demanded.

"She was going to kill you, that's what," Nicole said from the front porch. "I think the little hussy would have killed anyone who got between her and her get-rich scheme. Callie? Is that you?"

Callie came out from behind the bush. Nicole stared at her. "Did you break my windows?"

"I'm afraid so. I'll pay for them." Now she felt a little silly.

"Pay for them? Honey, you saved my life. That girl had blood lust in her eyes, she was so sure she had everything figured. But then the glass broke, and you shoulda seen her face. It was almost comical."

Tamra's gaze darted from one of her adversaries to another and back again. Suddenly she turned and bolted toward the street.

"Stop her!" Nicole cried. "She's a murderer. She killed your father, Sam."

Sam tensed, as if he might give chase.

"Let her go," Callie said. She could hear sirens. "She's running for her car parked at the end of the street, but she won't get far. Oh, dear. I think I need to sit down." Her knees had turned suddenly wobbly. She managed to teeter to the porch steps and sink down, hugging her knees. Of all things to think about at this moment, she was wondering if Sam would call off the wedding now that he knew that she'd continued to meddle behind his back.

Sam was looking at her in a way that worried her. His expression went beyond shock over learning about his father being murdered, or curiosity over her actions. He looked downright condemning.

Sam felt shaky himself. He hadn't really believed Tamra could pull the trigger when he'd taken the gun away from her. He hadn't believed she was a murderer. But with Callie and Nicole both claiming that was the case . . .

Damn. He'd known all along that something wasn't right about the suicide, but he'd swept his suspicions under the carpet rather than face them. Losing his father was hard enough without facing more controversy. He'd even silently condemned Callie for merely seeking the truth. What a fool he'd been, harboring a murderer in the family while turning a blind eye to the anomalies.

He sank onto Nicole's porch swing, feeling a little woozy. Though he was shocked at the idea that his father had been murdered by a member of his own family, it would also be a relief to know he hadn't killed himself.

His glance slid to Callie. She was safe, at least. That was a relief too. But beyond that, he couldn't name what he was feeling. Maybe he was in shock.

He watched with detachment as two police cars pulled up. Nicole seemed to be the only one of the three on the front porch who was up to taking any action. She ran up to the first car. "That woman running down the street," she screamed to the officer. "She tried to kill me!"

A third patrol car pulled up at the end of the street, blocking Tamra's escape. She fell onto her knees before anyone even attempted to capture her. A woman patrol officer got out of the car and went to Tamra, gently taking hold of her arm.

The officer wouldn't be that gentle, Sam thought, if

she'd seen the way Tamra had been flailing her pistol around.

The pistol was still in his hand, he realized. He laid it down beside him.

The uniformed officers asked a lot of questions. Nicole didn't exactly do herself credit with her screeching, hysterical recounting of Tamra's assault. They listened to Callie, though. They all knew her from the newspaper. She gave no more than a bare-bones account of following Tamra, witnessing the assault, and breaking the windows as a diversion. Sam couldn't add much more to the story except that he'd gotten a garbled, frightened message from Callie and had come looking for her.

When things started to calm down, he still said nothing to Callie about the job offers pouring in to her answering machine. Even if she wanted to turn her back on those opportunities, Sam knew he couldn't allow it. He couldn't let her . . .

Hell, since when had he ever been able to tell Callie what to do? She followed her own conscience, her own heart. No matter how much she loved him, she did what she thought was right, even if it went against his wishes.

Bennett showed up a few minutes later on a motorcycle, in street clothes. Sam didn't have the energy to feel even a little jealous. Besides, it was obvious that Callie had no romantic feelings for Sloan. Her gaze remained on Sam, her brown doe's eyes pleading with him to understand.

And, dammit, maybe he was just beginning to.

The aftermath took hours. Witnesses and suspects made statements at the scene, then were hustled down to police headquarters, where they made more statements. A reporter and photographer from the *Daily Record* showed up. Callie politely refused to make statements to her former coworkers. She wouldn't give Tom Winers a thing.

Not so Sam. Callie peered through a doorway at the police station, her jaw slack, watching as Sam cooperated fully with the reporter, discussing his and Tamra's roles in the recent drama, admitting that his father's death was still open to interpretation.

Callie would never have believed Sam would give any newspaper, especially the *Daily Record*, the time of day. He had to know that his family's name would be dragged through the mud again, even with the most tasteful coverage of this story—which she doubted he would get, knowing that Tom was still acting as editor.

And then he mentioned her name. She expected him to let her have it—at least to make some kind of snide comment about her rushing in where the police feared to tread, and all that. Instead, his comments were purely flattering. He painted her as an astute, concerned citizen, not a meddling ex-reporter sticking her nose where it didn't belong.

But what thoughts were brewing behind those steady blue eyes? He and Callie hadn't had a private moment between them since he'd arrived in town.

That moment came when, abruptly, all of the attention ceased. The press left. The police, having extracted every nuance from them, lost interest. Tamra was behind bars, for the moment. Focus turned to Johnny

Sanger's murder, and since Sam and Callie had already told as much as they knew on that subject, they were free to go.

Sloan Bennett borrowed a police cruiser and took them back to their cars. None of them could muster the energy for even pleasantries.

And then Sam and Callie were alone, standing by her Nissan. She opened the door and stood behind it, as if it could shield her from Sam's anger.

Only she wasn't sure if he was angry or just bewildered by her behavior. "I guess nothing I said to the police really explains what I was up to this afternoon, following Tamra around."

"Oh, I think I understand. You have a hard time leaving questions unanswered. You just couldn't let it go."

"I wanted to—"

"I wouldn't have expected you to. Your reporter's instinct is part of you, just like my ranching is a part of me. You're the one who explained that to me not so long ago. Only I didn't get it then. I do now."

"I wasn't acting as a reporter," Callie said, her chin jutting out defensively, though a tiny seed of hope blossomed inside her chest. Did Sam really understand? "I was helping the police. I had no intention of writing a story."

"No? Not even if it would get you a job with *The Washington Post?* Ah, hell, what am I saying? You don't need some sensational story to get a job. Seems every damn newspaper in the country wants you."

"Um . . . you found out about the *Post*."

"Yeah, and the *Miami Herald* and the *Dallas Morning*

News and the *Timbuktu Tribune*, probably. When were you going to tell me?"

"The *Timbuk*—Sam, what are you talking about?"

"The job offers. Coming in like cats from the rain. I . . . I listened to your answering-machine tape."

"You did what?" Her Sam had eavesdropped on her private telephone calls?

"I was there when that lady from the *Post* called. To talk about your job. And your ranch story. I let the answering machine get it, but then when she said the job was yours, I rewound the tape to listen again. Callie, I couldn't help it. I felt like I was seeing a secret life or something."

Callie didn't know how to respond to that accusation. It was true, to a degree, she supposed. "The *Miami Herald* really called?" she asked, focusing on the most minor of her concerns because it was easier.

"And the *Dallas Morning News* and some other big paper too. You're hot, Callie." Something flashed in his eyes, but it wasn't anger. Pain?

"I would have told you about the *Post* after the wedding," she answered.

"After . . . you were going to marry me and then move to D.C.?"

"No." She was amazed that he still didn't get it. "I was going to marry you and *not* move to D.C. I don't want to live in Washington. I want to marry you and live in Babcock, Nevada. And you were going to send me away." At this point she figured she better come clean about everything. "I was offered the *Post* job before I even left Washington."

"Then you lied the night . . . the night I proposed?"

She nodded miserably. "I was going to tell you about it, and tell you I'd already decided to turn down the job. And then you said you wouldn't marry me if I got the job, and I started thinking about how miserable I'd be in Washington waiting around for you to decide I loved you enough to make a commitment to you and Deana, or if you loved me enough to take a chance on me, and I just couldn't tell you."

Sometime during her long-winded confession, she'd started crying. And she'd ended up in Sam's arms, her face pressed against his chest.

"It's okay, Callie," he crooned. "I think I understand. I think. But what about all these job offers? Everyone wants you. How can I expect you to stop doing what you were meant to do? You can write your own ticket. I . . . I love you too much to hold you back."

She turned her tear-streaked face up to look at him. "I don't care if everyone else wants me. Only you. Do you want me?"

"It's not important—"

"Do you want me, Sam? Yes or no."

"Yes." He sounded pretty sure.

"Then I will write my own ticket. Callie Calloway Sanger, one one-way ticket to Babcock, Nevada, and Roundrock. I'm going to be a ranch wife and a mother and possibly a small-town newspaper publisher. 'Cause I couldn't love you more, Sam." He opened his mouth to object, but she forestalled him. "Before you even ask, yes, I'm sure. I've never been more sure about how I feel, or what to do with my life, not even when I was twenty years old and I thought I knew everything. Oh, and that ranch story—that's just something I spouted off the top of my head when Gloria asked me if I had any ideas. She was crazy about it, and I faxed her some stuff, but I wouldn't have pursued it without your permission. I know how you feel about the press."

He laughed, low and soft, and the sound soothed Callie's frazzled nerves. "For better or worse, I've committed myself to letting the press walk all over us. I figure the more we cooperate now, the sooner they'll get tired of us. One little story about my ranch couldn't possibly hurt anything."

"Really?" She couldn't believe her ears. "And what about the rest?"

"Your ticket, you mean?" He pulled her out from behind the car door and hugged her to him, giving her the gentlest of kisses. That was all the answer she needed.

Callie melted against him. For the first time in several hours she stopped feeling cold and frightened. Sam wanted her, despite the fact that she'd mismanaged everything. "Can we still be married right away?" she asked suddenly. "Maybe we should wait, given the fact that Tamra's in jail and your mother's going to be upset—"

"Mom would be more upset if we postponed the wedding. She's been talking about it nonstop ever since we announced our engagement. Let's go for it. Focusing on something happy will take everyone's minds off what's happened, at least for a while."

"I'm glad you feel that way. I don't think I could

wait another day, or a week or a month—and certainly not a year like you wanted to."

He pulled back and grinned at her. "I didn't really want to wait, you know."

Callie gazed back. Seeing the love, the utter confidence, shining from Sam's eyes, she knew they were making the right decision.

The times ahead weren't going to be easy; there would be Tamra's trial, and Beverly and Will would need all the emotional support she and Sam could spare. A long, hard winter awaited her at Roundrock, and she would have to learn to cope with snow and isolation.

But somehow, when she looked up into Sam's eager face, she knew without a doubt that they would make it. They were strong people individually. Together, they would be unbeatable.

"I don't think I've ever seen you with such a goofy smile," Sam said, kissing her forehead.

"I don't think I've ever felt so goofy in love," Callie replied. "C'mon, let's go home. I'll make you some soup out of a can. Hey, maybe Rena will teach me how to cook."

Sam opened the door of the Nissan and seated Callie behind the wheel like he was seating her in Cinderella's carriage. The gentle gesture warmed Callie from the inside out. She thought of all the times together that awaited them, the grand passions and the small, tender moments, and she knew she would never feel a moment's regret for choosing a life with Sam.

THE EDITORS' CORNER

Next month LOVESWEPT presents Men of Power. Whether they are scaling sheer rock walls, concealed by a mask of mystery, embroiled in white-hot desert seduction, or slipping in and out of the shadows of the night, these men will fulfill your wildest fantasies. So sit back and experience the supermen of November, as they battle for passion, love, and the promise of forever. You won't be disappointed.

SURRENDER THE SHADOW, LOVE-SWEPT #810, is another superb love story in Sandra Chastain's acclaimed MAC'S ANGELS series. No one can get in or out of dangerous places better than Connor Preston, the handsome enigma his Green Beret buddies nicknamed the Shadow, but Erica Fallon presents a different kind of threat! Once engaged to the brash daredevil, she'd vanished during a violent attack that shattered his world. Now they're reunited but their love must survive a mysterious menace. Get set for a page-turning read of erotic intrigue as only Sandra can tell it.

Award-winning author Donna Kauffman burns up the pages in **SANTERRA'S SIN**, LOVESWEPT #811. When she answers his knock with "Enter at your own risk," Diego Santerra realizes he has his hands full protecting Blue Delgado without her knowledge. He's taken more than a little pleasure keeping an eye on her the past three weeks, but now he has to get closer. That means getting a job at her cantina and running the risk of endangering his heart. At her best when the story sizzles, Donna will wow you with a hero born for trouble, and a lady strong enough to handle him!

From Riley Morse, one of our talented new discoveries, comes **THE LAST HONEST MAN**, LOVESWEPT #812. Jack Graham looks every inch a god as he fearlessly scales the wall of rock, while Hannah McKenzie watches in breathless wonder. No ordinary man can move that fast, or sense her presence so far away, but he has—and she feels the heat of his eyes brand her with uncivilized desire. Desperate to touch the woman who has breached his isolation, he dares to trust her with the shocking truth. Riley delivers a breath-stealing tale of fantasy and mystery.

WHEN NIGHT FALLS, LOVESWEPT #813, by acclaimed author Cheryln Biggs, is an invitation to venture into the shadowed reaches of the human heart. Scarred by tragedy and devastated by guilt, Anton Reichard has hidden himself deep in the Louisiana bayous running his empire with ruthless indifference—until reporter Dani Coroneaux penetrates his fortress! Vowing to get the story no one knows of the brooding maverick with the haunted gaze, Dani may prove to be Anton's sensual salvation. A stunning love story from an author already acclaimed for the intensity of her writing.

Happy reading!

With warmest wishes,

Beth de Guzman
Senior Editor

Shauna Summers
Editor

P.S. Watch for these Bantam women's fiction titles coming in November. From national bestseller Teresa Medeiros comes **SHADOWS AND LACE**, a captivating medieval love story rich in humor and passion. When Rowena's drunken father loses her to the service of a forbidding knight accused of murder, the Dark Lord of Caerleon thinks he can use her to slay the ghosts of his past. But soon he will be ensnared by his own trap—slave to a desire he can never hope to quench. In **THE MARRIAGE WAGER**, by Jane Ashford, Lady Emma Tarrant had watched her husband gamble his life away and now she's determined to save another young man from a similar fate. So she challenges Colin Wareham, the scoundrel who holds the young man's debts, to another game. Intrigued, he names his stakes: a loss, and he forgives the debts. A win, and the lady must give him her heart.

Don't miss the previews of these exceptional novels in next month's LOVESWEPTs. And immediately following this page, sneak a peek at the Bantam women's fiction titles on sale now!

Don't miss these extraordinary books
by your favorite Bantam authors

On sale in September

TAME THE WILD WIND
by Rosanne Bittner

BETROTHED
by Elizabeth Elliott

Rosanne Bittner

mistress of romantic frontier fiction

TAME THE WILD WIND

A tale as wide and free as the passion
of the human heart

*Half-breed Gabe Beaumont had had to choose between the
Sioux tribe of his mother and the white family of his father, and his choice had cost him everything. Settlers murdered his Indian wife and child, leaving him with a grief
that filled his soul with anger . . . until he met Faith
Kelley, a feisty, red-haired beauty who had faced her own
tragedy and rebuilt her life around a lonely stage stop that
had become her home. But when the stage stop and everything Faith has worked for fall under attack by a renegade
Sioux band, she never suspects that the leader of the Indian
raid will return later as a darkly handsome cowboy, a man
who changed worlds to claim the woman who is his
destiny. . . .*

"Tall Bear," she whispered. He had come back! She
moved to the door. "Tall Bear? Is that you out
there?"

"It is," came the reply.

Why had he come back? Whatever the reason, she

needed help. She lifted away the bar across the door and stepped back. "Come in," she called to him.

The door opened, and Tall Bear walked inside to see Faith holding a rifle on him. He closed the door, standing there quietly, not surprised she still did not trust him.

Faith stared at him in surprise. He was washed and shaved, and he had cut his hair to shoulder length. He was wearing dark cotton pants, leather boots, a white man's yellow slicker, and a leather hat. Through the open front of the slicker she could see he wore a six-gun belted to his hip, and she saw a dark shirt and a short wool jacket. He was dressed totally as a white man.

"Tall Bear! What on earth—where did you come from? Where have you been? Why are you—"

"I have decided I will stay and work for you," he interrupted. How could he tell her the truth—that she had haunted his dreams? How could he tell her the reason he left the first time was because he was afraid of his own feelings for this feisty, independent woman—a woman far removed from one who would be interested in a half-breed who had not only raided and killed with the Sioux but also with white outlaws. Still, he had not been able to stay away, and the fact remained he needed honest work.

Faith stepped back, lowering her rifle, and Tall Bear thought she looked upset. "I am sorry. I thought you would still want me here to help. If you want me to go, I will go."

Faith blinked back tears. "It isn't that. I—" She glanced over at Johnny. "It's just that I can't talk about this right now. I can't make any decisions." She moved her gaze back to Tall Bear. "Actually, for the moment you couldn't have come at a better time. I'm scared, Tall Bear. My son is very sick. I'm afraid—" The words caught in her throat, and she felt so helpless. "I'm afraid he's dying." She choked in a sudden sob and covered her mouth, letting the tears flow. In the next moment she felt a hand on her shoulder, and she was resting her head against his chest and crying.

It seemed so natural. Never had Faith been so aware that she needed to be held, needed someone else's strength. She realized with overwhelming starkness that she had needed this for months, maybe for years. Her father had never held her lovingly or with any sense of true support. Nor had Johnny. The only time Johnny had held her was when he wanted sex. In Tall Bear's arms she felt the first real comfort she had known other than when her own mother had embraced her. She felt a sudden wave of relief, as though his presence meant everything would be all right. It seemed silly to think so, but his embrace was firm and warm, and she sensed the sincerity in the gesture.

"I don't know what to do, Tall Bear. He has a terrible fever and cough, and he's so listless. He looks at me as though he doesn't even know me."

She felt him removing the rifle from her hand, and she did not object. "Come," he told her. "We will see what we can do for him."

He led her over to the cot and leaned over Johnny, removing the blanket from around him and feeling his hot skin. "You are right," he told her. "This is bad. You must cool him down right away or he will die."

Faith wiped at tears. "I—I thought I should keep him wrapped tight, make him sweat it out."

He shook his head. "No. You must remove his clothing and immerse him in cool water. You must bring the fever down or it will affect his brain. While you do that I must leave. I will bring something back with me that will help. While I am gone, put a pan of water on the cookstove and heat it."

"No, don't leave me here alone! You won't come back."

"I promise that I will. I already came back once, didn't I?" He grasped her arms, forcing her to meet his gaze.

Faith saw truth there in his exotic green eyes. She was too concerned with Johnny to truly notice him the way a woman should notice a man like this, but somewhere deep inside the woman in her did notice, and she liked what she saw. "What will you get?"

"It is an old Indian remedy. You must trust me. I have caused you enough hurt. I would not lie to you about this. Get your son into cool water right away, then wrap him again as soon as he is out so that he does not shiver with chill. Heat the pan of water. I will be back soon." He grabbed his hat and slicker again, leaving the jacket behind as he left without further explanation. Faith ran to the window and opened the shutters to see him riding away. He had left behind his pack horse, which satisfied her worry he would not return. She felt sorry for him riding off into the cold rain, but if it was for something that would help Johnny, then so be it.

She quickly set a wash pan on the stove, then poured already-heated water from the kettle into the pan, building up the fire under the burner to keep the water in both vessels hot. Next she took down a washtub that hung on a wall and set it beside Johnny's cot. She poured two buckets of water into it, praying Tall Bear was right about how to bring down the fever. It just didn't seem safe to put Johnny's little fevered body into cool water. She would never have thought to do such a thing, afraid it would kill him, but if this was something the Sioux had always done, perhaps there was some use to it. After all, they were a people who had to survive out here with no white man's help, no doctors, no fancy potions and creams. She remembered Buck saying once that the Indians had their own kind of medicine and seemed to do "right good" at treating their own sicknesses.

What other choice did she have? To leave things as they were would surely mean Johnny's death. She unwrapped him, and he made only a little whimpering sound as she undressed him. It was as though he did not have the energy to cry. Perhaps he had a sore throat on top of the fever and congestion. Perhaps he simply could not get enough air to cry. His little head rolled back and his arms hung limp when she picked him up, but his body jerked when she set him in the cool water. He made another whimpering sound.

"I'm sorry, Johnny, but Mommy is only trying to do what's best for you." She cupped water in her hand and began pouring it over his forehead to cool his face and neck. After a few minutes he seemed to become more alert. He kicked and splashed water, then began the awful coughing again, so fierce she was sure he would choke to death on phlegm or die simply from the inability to draw enough air into his congested lungs. "Please hurry, Tall Bear," she prayed, still terrified for her little boy.

After about twenty more minutes she finally heard him returning. He came through the door, his big frame seeming to fill the room. He held what looked like pieces of bark in his hands, and he set them on the table, then removed his wet slicker and his hat, hanging both things on the wall. Faith noticed that without the extra coats he still seemed intimidating in size, and he still wore the six-gun.

"I have brought the bark of red cedar," he told her. "I will boil it in the water. As soon as it releases its oils, I will take Johnny over to the boiling water and put a blanket over us. You will have to watch the blanket to be sure it does not get near open flame. I need to make a kind of tent over us so that your son breathes the steam from the bark. It will help clear his lungs. My people have used this for many generations to chase away the lung sickness."

Faith clung to Johnny. "Does it always work?"

He walked over and broke the bark into little pieces, placing them into the wash pan, which was already steaming. "Most of the time."

"*Most* of the time?"

He poured more water from the kettle into the pan. "Nothing in this life is sure. I only know this usually helps. The rest is in God's hands."

She thought it strange he should say that, as though he believed in her God. The room was silent for the next few minutes. Faith continued to rock Johnny, and Tall Bear poked at the bark, stirring it a little. He leaned down, sniffed it, and after several minutes he told her to bring the boy to him, along with an extra blanket. Faith decided she had no choice but to trust him.

She carried the baby to Tall Bear, their gaze holding as she handed him over. "He's all I have," she reminded him.

"I know the feeling of loving a son," he answered, taking the boy into his arms, "and how it feels to lose one to death."

She saw the pain in his eyes. "I'm sorry. I'm thinking only of myself and my own son."

"That is as it should be. Put the extra blanket over my head. Once the water in the pan is boiling hard I will take him over and sit on the cot with him. You can carry the pan and set it on the floor and we will continue to sit over the steam, using the blanket to hold it in."

For several minutes Tall Bear held the boy over the water, and she thought how he must be getting hot and sweaty under there himself, and that his arms must be getting tired from holding Johnny, but he hardly moved. Finally Johnny began coughing again. He gagged, and she heard Tall Bear pounding on his back. He told her then to quickly bring the pan over to the cot, and he carried Johnny there, sitting down on the edge. He talked to the boy softly in the Sioux tongue, and Faith was amazed the boy was not crying at being held by a stranger, such a big, intimidating man at that, a man he'd seen attack the station only a month ago. On top of that, Tall Bear was talking to him in a strange language. Perhaps the boy was simply too dazed to understand what was happening to him.

"I'm sorry you have to sit under there like that,"

she told Tall Bear. "I can sit with him for a while if you want."

"I am fine," he told her. "I have sat in the sweat lodge many times for purification. It is much hotter than this. It is good for the lungs, and good for the soul."

Minutes seemed like hours, and finally a good hour did pass before she heard Johnny speak. "Ta Baew," he said. Her heart leaped with joy at the words.

"No," Tall Bear answered. "That is no longer my name, Johnny. I am Gabe. Can you say Gabe?"

"Gabe," the boy said after a moment.

"An exciting find for romance readers everywhere!"
—Amanda Quick, *New York Times* bestselling author

Elizabeth Elliott

BETROTHED

Guy of Montague rode into Lonsdale Castle to reclaim Halford Hall, only to be enchanted by Claudia, Baron Lonsdale's beautiful niece. Then her uncle sets a trap and Guy is forced into a betrothal with Claudia, who is being held captive until the marriage ceremony. Claudia comes to his rescue, but on the condition that he take her with him. But Guy finds himself under her spell. He will risk everything, even his life, to capture Claudia's heart. . . .

Guy gestured toward the marble bench that sat beneath the rose arbor. "Will you sit with me?"

She took an involuntary step backward. "I—I have work to do."

She didn't take the hand he offered, but she did make her way to the bench and sat down. No good could come of this, yet it wasn't fear that made her heart beat faster. It was the man who walked toward her.

He sat beside her without asking permission, his movements smooth and unhurried. "I was surprised when I did not see you at mass. Tell me you are not a pagan, or excommunicated for some dire reason."

"I attended mass this morning," she informed him

in a prim voice. Her brows drew together in a frown. "You looked for me at mass?"

"I searched for you everywhere." He said that with such ease that she felt certain he teased her. He studied her face for a moment and seemed to read her thoughts. "You do not believe me?"

The exaggerated look he gave her was one of such wounded feelings that she smiled, aware that she smiled into the face of danger. This one could charm snakes, should he put his mind to it. "You cannot search for someone you do not know, baron."

"I know more about you than you might think. You are only half Italian, on your father's side, and your mother was Baron Lonsdale's sister. Five years ago, you and two brothers came to England after the deaths of your parents. Your brothers left soon after, but you remained at Lonsdale and earn your keep as a seamstress. 'Tis all I know of you at present, yet I would like to know more. Much more."

His gaze moved over her face and settled on her mouth. Probably because it hung wide open. She snapped it shut. "How do you know so much about me?"

"It is in my best interests to know everything I can about Baron Lonsdale and his family. I came here to make a contract with your uncle, and I never enter into a contract without knowing all I can of whom I bargain with." He propped his hands at the edge of the bench behind him and stretched out his legs to cross them at the ankle.

"I also know that you and your uncle are not close. Why does he dislike you?"

She began to brush at a few smudges of dirt on

her gown. "My grandfather arranged my mother's marriage to a man Uncle Laurence never liked. He says I am the image of my father in looks and temperament." She concentrated on a grass stain, unable to look him in the eye but willing to repay his honesty. "I do not speak your language as well as I should after five years in this country. My uncle says it offends him even when I speak, that he must hear my father as well as look upon him whenever I enter a room. 'Dislike' is a mild word to describe what my uncle feels for me."

He said nothing for a long time. She'd probably disgusted him by blurting out her family problems.

"Your life here must be very difficult, Lady Claudia."

His voice was so soft, so very gentle that she wanted to cry. She forced a smile instead and gazed out over the gardens. " 'Tis not so bad. Lonsdale is a large fortress, and I can avoid my uncle's company most of the time. Indeed, there are days when I believe he forgets I exist."

"But you would rather live somewhere else?"

That remark made her think of her brother Dante, of the fine Welsh keep he mentioned in his last missive. If all went well with Dante, someday she would have a garden of her own, in a home where she could be happy again. "Yes, I would rather live somewhere else."

He startled her when he placed his fingertips beneath her chin and turned her face toward his. "Do you have a suitor, Lady Claudia? Some man who longs to make you his wife?"

She laughed aloud. "Nay, baron. I doubt any man

in England longs for one such as me. Most can understand no more than one of every three words I speak, and I am beyond the age when most maids marry." She shook her head and held her hands with the palms upward to show them empty. "Most men long for a wealthy heiress, but what you see here is my dowry. Only a fool would wish for such a wife."

His expression grew more intense. "I am well acquainted with a fool."

She didn't know what to make of that strange remark, nor what to do when he gathered his legs beneath him and moved toward her. "What are you doing, baron?"

"I would like you to call me by my given name." He leaned closer, his eyes as deep and mysterious as a fathomless sea.

Panic rose fast inside her. She slid away until she sat on the edge of the bench, but had to lay her palm against his chest to hold him at bay. "You should not look at me this way, baron!"

"Guy." He captured her hand beneath his and held it against his heart. "My name is Guy."

The moment he touched her hand, Claudia forgot why she'd placed it there in the first place. She felt dizzy and disoriented, as if every thought had suddenly emptied itself from her head. He continued to move toward her, yet she didn't realize his intent until his lips touched hers. And still he watched her, with eyes that had somehow turned to blue fire.

Claudia didn't know what to do. She closed her eyes. That didn't help. If one strong arm hadn't wrapped itself around her, she would have fallen off the edge of the bench. She was soon surrounded by his warmth. His lips began to move against hers, brushing back and forth but never leaving her, pressing closer and closer until her mouth was moving with his and against it at the same time. No man had ever kissed her, although she'd sometimes wondered what it would be like. Now she knew. It was like being drunk on thin air. She wanted it to go on forever. It seemed as if it would. She wanted—

She was sitting on his lap!

Claudia stiffened and tried to push away from him. "Baron! Y—you forget yourself!"

"Guy," he murmured, pressing one last, lingering kiss on her lips. He lifted his head and looked into her eyes, as if he were searching for something. At last he smiled. "You must learn to call me Guy." She tried to scoot off his lap, but his grip on her tightened. "Hold very still, Claudia."

"Release me, baron."

He shook his head. "Never."

She tried not to panic. He'd turned into a madman. A lust-crazed madman. That was the source of the strange light in his eyes. Before they kissed that light had fascinated her. Now it frightened her. She lifted her hand and slapped him, not hard, but hopefully hard enough to bring him to his senses.

Guy blinked once very slowly. When he opened his eyes again, they no longer burned with passion. He looked confused. "Why did you do that?"

"Why did I—" Claudia pressed her palm to her own cheek and released a shaky sigh. He was woodenheaded as well as crazed. "I thought it might return you to your senses, baron. You did not come here to kiss me."

He lifted one hand to her temple and his gaze moved to the stray wisp of hair that he rubbed between his fingers. "I suspected rightly enough that you wanted to kiss me. There seemed no reason to delay the matter."

Claudia pulled the lock of hair from his grasp and tucked it behind her ear in one harsh movement. He looked as if she'd just slapped him again. "I don't know why I let you kiss me, but it will not happen again. What we did—what you are doing now is . . . is sinful."

"Perhaps." He didn't look the least disturbed by the possibility. "Perhaps not.

"Was that your first kiss?"

"Aye."

He lifted her hand and pressed another sensuous kiss against her wrist. "Good. I hoped I would be the first." He glanced toward the path that led to the bailey and his mouth became a straight line. "I must leave you, Claudia. 'Tis unlikely we will have another opportunity to speak alone again before tomorrow." His lips brushed against hers in a kiss so brief that it was over almost before she realized it had begun. "Do not kiss anyone else until then. I want you to save your kisses for me."

DON'T MISS THESE FABULOUS BANTAM WOMEN'S FICTION TITLES

On Sale in September

TAME THE WILD WIND

by ROSANNE BITTNER

the mistress of romantic frontier fiction

Here is the sweeping romance
of a determined woman who runs a stagecoach inn
and the half-breed who changes worlds to
claim the woman he loves.

_____ 56996-1 $5.99/$7.99 in Canada

BETROTHED

by ELIZABETH ELLIOTT

"An exciting find for romance readers everywhere!"
—AMANDA QUICK,
New York Times bestselling author

Guy of Montague rides into Lonsdale Castle to
reclaim Halford Hall, only to be forced into a
betrothal with the baron's beautiful niece.

_____ 57566-X $5.50/$7.50 in Canada

- -

Ask for these books at your local bookstore or use this page to order.

Please send me the books I have checked above. I am enclosing $_____ (add $2.50 to
cover postage and handling). Send check or money order, no cash or C.O.D.'s, please.

Name _____

Address _____

City/State/Zip _____

Send order to: Bantam Books, Dept. FN159, 2451 S. Wolf Rd., Des Plaines, IL 60018
Allow four to six weeks for delivery.
Prices and availability subject to change without notice.   FN 159 9/96